Michael R. Davidson

eye for an eye

By

Michael R. Davidson

Michael R. Davidson

eye for an eye

Copyright © 2015 by Michael R. Davidson

MRD Enterprises, Inc.
PO BOX 1000
Mount Jackson, VA 22842-1000
mrdenter@shentel.net

Library of Congress Control Number: Pending
ISBN: 978-0-578-16756-5

Cover Design by Michael R. Davidson
Photo: CamStockPhoto, Inc.
Zürich Map from Rough Guides, Switzerland.isyours.com
London Map from ToursofLondon
Map of Switzerland from CIA Maps

Printed and bound in the United States of America.

First printing 2015

Michael R. Davidson

This is a work of fiction and the situations described, as well as the characters and their actions are totally imaginary.

The author is a former officer of the Central Intelligence Agency's Clandestine Services and is therefore required to provide the following statement:

"Having reviewed the manuscript, as required by law, the CIA instructs that the following statement be made: "All statements of act, opinion, or analysis expressed are those of the author and do not reflect the official positions or views of the CIA or any other U.S. Government agency. Nothing in the contents should be construed as asserting or implying U.S. Government authentication of information or Agency endorsement of the author's views. This material has been reviewed by the CIA to prevent the disclosure of classified information."

Acknowledgments:

I completed the original manuscript of this story several years ago. It was meant to be a sequel to "Harry's Rules." (And so it still is.) But my agent at the time, the dear departed John Hawkins, and I thought it needed more work. I laid it aside in favor of "Incubus," which I already had begun, and the story has remained dormant ever since.

I recently dusted off this manuscript and decided to cut out more than half of the original text, eliminate many characters and sub-plots

With some trepidation I submitted the revised manuscript to my friend and fellow author Clabe Taylor, who patiently waded through several iterations. Many thanks to Clabe for his sage advice.

Also, many thanks to John Eldred for his willingness to check for typos.

"The Incubus Vendetta" took Harry Connolly aka Ewan Ramsay and the fearsome Sasha off into the mists of retirement, but **"eye for an eye"** brings them back to the early days, in the 90's and pits them once again against their arch-enemy, Vitaliy Mikhailovich Shurgin. Shurgin's ally, the malevolent mafioso "Zhenya" Lomonosov also makes another appearance and proves just how dangerous he is.

New Market, Va 2015

Michael R. Davidson

ZÜRICH

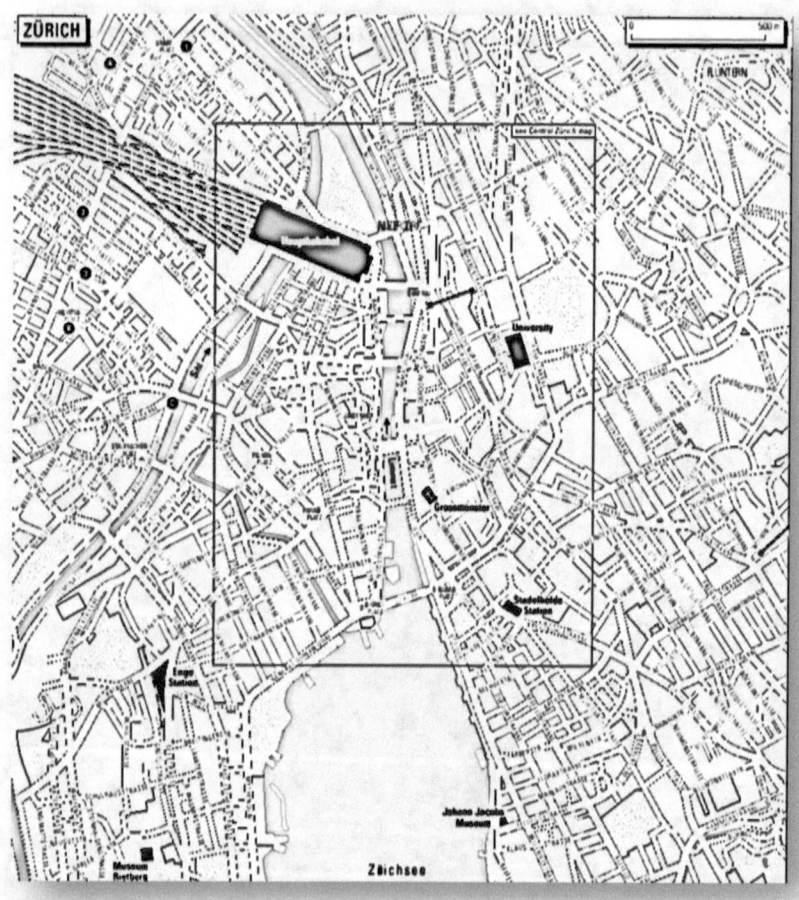

Vengeance in Russia does not belong to the Lord. Long ago Russians took God into their homes and made of him a pet to hang on the wall, and they prayed to him to destroy their enemies.

It's a country where distrust is instinctual and whose inhabitants have learned at great cost that faith in one's fellow man is a foolish notion. Russians do not turn the other cheek. Russians do not forgive their enemies. And if there isn't an enemy in sight, they will be sure to create one.

"I like the idea of a fishing expedition," said one of the men, the large one.

"We'll dangle someone they should know is involved," agreed the other, the slender, foxlike one with red hair. "Let's see what kind of fish rises to the bait."

Michael R. Davidson

Prologue

VILLA OF "ZHENYA" LOMONOSOV
ZÜRICH, SWITZERLAND

The naked man huddled in the corner of the cell. He whimpered with anticipated pain when the bright light recessed into the ceiling flashed on. His entire existence now was circumscribed by pain – remembered pain, present pain, and imagined pain triangulated on his being.

The reason had been explained clearly to him, but it was ridiculous – totally incongruous with the virtuous life he had led. It was so unfair! He definitely did not deserve this. He had just tried to do the right thing. All he had at the moment were questions and regret ... and the pain.

His life had become a zero sum game which began that day when the inspector from the Swiss Bundespolizei (BUPO), the federal internal security police, arrived unannounced at his bank office for a "private conversation."

Yes, that was the *beginning*.

In his position as Deputy Director of his bank, the Inspector said, he must be aware of the activities of his clients. As a patriotic, law-abiding Swiss citizen, he must also be aware that he had a duty to report unlawful activities.

Did he know of a certain Yevgeniy Lomonosov, a Russian currently residing in Zürich?

Of course the Deputy Director knew who Lomonosov was: a fabulously wealthy man, one of the so-called Russian "oligarchs" who had found clever ways to capitalize on the chaotic economic situation in post-soviet Russia.

"You know I am not permitted to divulge private information on bank clients," he had insisted.

"But some of the pertinent laws in that regard have changed," replied the inspector, who exploited every advantage. He appealed to the banker's patriotism. Lomonosov was a very bad guy, he explained, a Russian Mafioso.

The money he spread around from his enormous villa above the *Zürichsee* served to legitimize him so far as the public was concerned, unaware or uncaring of his past. BUPO, on the other hand, was very concerned. The Inspector referred to Lomonosov as a "chocolate covered turd."

The banker too late realized he should have adhered to the traditional practice of his breed, listened politely, and sent the cop on his way. Instead, to his certain regret, he chose an oblique alternative to avoid answering and said he would "think about it." That was all. Just three words. Even now he couldn't imagine that he would have spent another moment on the subject.

Unfortunately, one of Lomonosov's spies inside BUPO learned of the meeting and the banker's ambiguous response. Lomonosov's list of preferred qualities for Swiss bankers did not include ambiguity, and he never gave second chances.

On his way home from work a few days after the interview, the banker's car had been forced off the road. Before he had time to react three armed men had yanked him out, placed a canvas bag over his head, bound him and tossed him roughly into the back of a white van and inserted a hypodermic syringe into his arm.

When he regained consciousness the first thing he saw was himself. The sensation was surreal, as though he were having an out of body experience. Then he realized that a mirror was mounted directly above him. The reflected image was of a plump man stripped naked and strapped tightly full length to a metal table. He could feel the straps biting into his flesh and the cold metal beneath him. He could not move a muscle. There was even a strap holding his head immobile.

The top of a man's head moved into the reflection. It was a man with closely cropped blond hair. The atmosphere of the room itself reminded him vaguely of a doctor's examining room, but the coppery smell was unfamiliar.

A noise caused him to turn his eyes upward again and he saw that a second man was setting up a video recording device on a tripod at a high angle above the foot of the table. *Some kind of sick porno?* The thought flashed through the banker's mind. *Did they plan to blackmail him?* The blond man didn't utter a word at first, but pulled on a rubber apron and gloves and then stood gazing appraisingly at the banker.

He moved out of the banker's vision for a moment then returned and held a scalpel close before the banker's eyes. In German, he said, "Trust and loyalty are very important to Herr Lomonosov. You thought to betray him. Now you must pay the price." Nodding toward the video camera, he continued, "but you will serve a good purpose in the end. You will be an example for others who might ever consider betrayal."

The banker protested. He had *not* betrayed his client. He would *never* do so. The blond man paid no attention. Instead, he went to work on the banker with the scalpel, slicing here, touching a nerve there. The ingeniousness and horror of the mirror were that the banker could discern every detail of what was done to him, as his own blood began to stream in rivulets across his reflected image and fill the recessed groove in the center of the operating table, finally disappearing down a drain at its foot. His screams echoed off the walls until the banker lost consciousness again.

The blond man waited for him to revive, and then continued with the scalpel, always careful to inflict maximum pain but no fatal damage. This went on for over an hour after which the bloody, but still living banker was tossed into a windowless cell. The process was repeated several times. The blond man was always careful to keep him alive. The video camera continued to record, and the mirrored image of his own agony burned into the banker's eyes.

*****

The light in the banker's cell flashed to life, and he heard a key turn in the lock in the heavy wooden door. When it opened he cringed, pressing his back into the wall.

The sadist, the torturer, the man with the hard, impassive eyes and no pity!

"Get up," he ordered, "We're taking you home."

Hope blossomed, a small flower fragile in its youth. The blond man lifted him to his feet and shoved him towards the door. "We are satisfied that you betrayed no secrets. We must treat your unfortunate wounds. You'll get dressed, and then we'll go."

Nearly unable to walk, the banker stumbled into the hallway grasping for support against the wall and managed somehow to put one foot ahead of the other, some feeble strength returned to him by the promise of release. Behind him, the blond man removed a pistol from his belt and fired a nine millimeter bullet into the back of the banker's skull, killing him instantly. The body would be disposed of that same night, transported to a deserted spot in the countryside and buried where it would never be found.

The next day the blond man, whose name was Ivan Dimov, knocked softly at the entrance to

Michael R. Davidson

Yevgeniy Lomonosov's study. He was dressed casually in dark wool slacks and a light cotton turtleneck sweater that hugged his well-muscled body. At 49 years old, he retained the strength and agility of a much younger man. His bearing was unmistakably military, although his training had taught him to disguise this when necessary. Within the confines of Lomonosov's well-protected grounds, he saw no reason to hide what he was.

There was a buzz, and the armored double doors controlled by hidden servos in the wall swung open. Lomonosov, known in the Russian underworld as Zhenya, leader of the most vicious criminal gang in Russia, "the *Bratsvo*[1]," greeted him from behind his ornate desk. Behind him, through the bulletproof glass of a large window, one could glimpse the *Zürichsee* in the distance over the church spires and the University of Zürich campus.

Zhenya's spare frame was impeccably draped, as usual, in one of his expensive bespoke suits, soft Egyptian cotton shirt, and Hermés tie. His appearance was reminiscent of the Prince of Wales until one noticed the unwavering, frigid stare of his arctic blue eyes. Under the splendid clothing and *faux* noble bearing lay the empty soul of a merciless beast, a tested and true *vor v*

---

[1] Brotherhood

zakonye, a "thief in the code" in the jargon of the violent Russian underworld. Zhenya controlled a far-flung criminal empire stretching from Moscow, to Miami, to Geneva, and as far distant as the Near East. His organization controlled money laundering, drug trafficking, sex slave trafficking, and owned interests in several well-known "legitimate" businesses, as well.

Zhenya was also an important part of *Voskreseniye Rossii ,* Russian Rebirth[2]. One hand washed the other with the *Bratsvo* providing money laundering and investment services for *Voskreseniye* and the latter, with its SVR network able to provide Zhenya's people with expertly forged documents and access to diplomatic pouches – capabilities that made Zhenya's criminal operations practically invulnerable to law enforcement detection. One would never say it was a marriage made in Heaven, but it was a mutually beneficial marriage nonetheless.

Following the collapse of the USSR, and especially in the wake of the unsuccessful 1991 coup against Gorbachev, instigated by Vladimir Kryuchkov, then Chairman of the KGB, the Soviet Union's intelligence and security services had been broken up, and many highly skilled former

---

[2] For a full explanation of the organization, see HARRY'S RULES and THE INCUBUS VENDETTA.

Michael R. Davidson

KGB officials now populated Zhenya's network – he would never know how many of them actually worked for him and how many still worked for Moscow Center, but he wasn't concerned.

Zhenya gestured for Dimov to take a seat. "I received a communication from the Center this morning." Zhenya enjoyed using KGB jargon, a relatively new and titillating experience. "You have new orders from Morozov."

Dimov waited. He had his own means of clandestine communication with General Morozov via a special *Spetsgruppa Vympel* network and had been alerted to expect orders.

Lomonosov continued, "You are to proceed immediately to London where you will link up with a local contact who will assist you." He pointed a manicured finger at a sheet of paper in the middle of his desk. "Your contact instructions and operational details."

Four hours later Dimov was aboard Zhenya's private jet on his way to Heathrow.

Chapter 1

CLEGGAN, IRELAND
LATE SPRING 1993

Intelligence work gets into your blood, shapes the way you look at the world. It can inoculate you against certain of life's pitfalls and make you untrusting of your fellow man.

For practitioners of espionage, subterfuge and distrust are second nature, as is subordination to the orders of one's service. Intelligence officers are a specific *type* with certain universal characteristics, often shaped by ideology. Thus love affairs are problematic – smoke in the eyes, as the old song goes.

Michael R. Davidson

The tall man pondered the conundrum as the jet black dog trotted at his side. Occasionally, the Scottie's almond shaped brown eyes turned up briefly toward his master but returned immediately to his hunt for unwary plover.

Both man and dog enjoyed their bog land walks. The man wore hiking boots, an olive drab Barbour Beaufort hunting jacket, and an old pair of brown corduroy trousers. He was tall and lean, and he had let his brown, slightly graying hair grow moderately long. People thought he bore a resemblance to the actor Clint Eastwood, something the man himself did not see. The man was a pariah, an international fugitive from the law, and a target for some very persistent Russians who wanted him dead.

He resided on the west coast of Ireland under a solidly established alias, and his life was comfortable thanks to the largess of a grateful Israeli government. The Mossad expected him to do them the occasional favor, especially whenever they came across a tasty Russian lead. So life remained interesting, and therefore good. The reason for his present philosophical fugue was Aleksandra Sergeyevna Turmarkina. Sasha, as she was known to her friends, was a Mossad operative with whom he had become much more than just friends.

Sasha had called earlier in the day from Shannon International Airport to inform him she needed some help on an assignment and was now making her way over the tedious drive northward through Galway and then west over increasingly narrow roads to Clifden up through Connemara before getting here. The best part was that she would spend the night. That left several hours to kill, and he had driven across the peninsula down toward Ballyconneely Bay and out into the bog lands of the High Moors to give his five year old Scots Terrier, Angus, a chance to run and stretch his legs.

Late Spring leaned hesitantly toward Summer, and the bogs were abloom. The Sphagnum mosses that have through the millennia decayed to form the peat commonly used for fuel in this part of Ireland had assumed their burgundy and orange hue, and the greens and pinks of the heaths and heathers combined with other vegetation to present an attractively carpeted landscape, dotted here and there with the white flowers of the bog bean. As is the wont of Scotties, Angus coursed through the low lying vegetation at top speed, his surprisingly big feet, attached to his body by short, but sturdy legs, seldom touching the ground, making wide circles around Ewan Ramsay as he hiked across the bog.

After an hour Ramsay boosted an exhausted but happy dog into his black Land Rover Defender and headed home. Home was just outside of Cleggan in Galway. Built of white native stone and brick with a slate roof, the single story three-bedroom house perched directly on a rocky promontory that jutted into Cleggan Bay, affording a spectacular view of the bay and the broad Atlantic beyond. The house boasted its own private cove and dock, and Ewan was considering whether he should purchase a boat. He knew nothing about boats, but the idea had appeal.

Chapter 2

SASHA

In the early afternoon the crunch of gravel in the drive signaled her arrival, and Ewan stepped out to greet her. She wore a white cotton sweater, jeans and boots, and had pulled her hair back in a ponytail, a contrast from the very proper *fraulein* he had first encountered in Vienna the previous year. He liked this version better.

She had become his point of reference in a whirlwind. She had been there from the beginning in Vienna when his previous existence disintegrated and the new one began. His alpha and omega.

Michael R. Davidson

She returned his smile but avoided the kiss he would have preferred, instead pressing her cheek to his as he gave her a welcoming hug. He held her at arm's length and surveyed her face. What was it in those hazel eyes, fear, hesitation, uncertainty? But then, she had made the trip to see him. In sum, the balance was positive.

It was like this with all of her visits. An initial hesitation. It always required time and patience for her to relax, to lock the Mossad outside the door. He had learned to get in synch with her, like a musician learning a new tune.

He took a step back and looked her up and down. "Have you gained weight?"

Nonplussed by the question, she gaped in surprise.

"That got your attention, didn't it?" And he laughed out loud at her momentary discomfiture.

Her response was to punch him in the chest.

With a look of agony he clutched the spot where her fist had landed and gasped, "That's right where I was shot!"

She was immediately contrite. "Oh, God, how bad is it?"

With which he doubled over in laughter. She punched him again, this time in the arm, and none too lightly. "You idiot."

The ice was broken. They were in synch, and she gave him a proper kiss.

Ewan's newly honed culinary skills combined with simple, good quality ingredients to guarantee that dinner was a success. Sasha's early years in the Soviet Union and then living with her widowed mother in Israel had not included gourmet cooking. Russian daily fair was notoriously bland – lots of cabbage and potatoes and dried fish.

The rest of the evening was satisfyingly recreational. As she peaked she only trembled and expelled a soft sigh, and he was overcome by tenderness.

They rolled onto their backs on the queen-sized bed, the only light coming from the warm glow of the peat bricks burning in the fireplace spreading their sweet aroma throughout the room to dispel the chill night air from the windows open to the crashing of the sea. He caressed the down on her flat stomach. "Are you ready for the QUESTION?"

She turned to look at him, a lock of ash blond hair drooping over one eye. "Mmmm, that feels good. Why don't we just keep conversation to a minimum?"

Not a bad answer, he thought.

He pulled her to him and pressed his lips to hers as he ran his fingers through her long hair.

Her tongue flicked playfully just inside his lips. As they made love, she murmured sweet sounding words in Hebrew that Ewan did not recognize.

They remained in the comfort of their embrace for a long moment before finally rolling again onto their backs, the glow from the fireplace reflected on the light sheen of perspiration that now covered their bodies. Finally he said, "OK, NOW may I ask the QUESTION?"

Her voice was soft, but firm, "The answer is the same. You know I can't do it, at least not now."

"Hmmm," he said, "You just did it very well … twice!"

She reached over and swatted him on the head. "You know what I mean," she said. "You're asking me to become a normal person, whatever that is. I've not been 'normal' since I was 12 years old. I've lived so long with impermanence, and layers and layers of secrecy, and alias identities have been my shield. It's hard just to set that all aside, to feel safe."

They shared a difficult long distance relationship. Sasha lived in Vienna under cover as manager of a small import-export company. Her status as a Mossad operative was very important to her. Should they marry, that status would be in jeopardy, would almost certainly end, and she was reluctant to part ways with the organization and the people that had been her life.

It was not that she did not trust Ewan; she did not yet fully trust her own emotions or where they might take her. Thank God he was so patient. She knew that she would not have been. He'd once remarked that getting two spooks together was like putting two porcupines in a box. It required careful adjustment.

Ramsay's feelings had overtaken him quite by stealth and grew each of the rare times they were together. He reasoned that in part it was because of his separation from all he had known, his own country included, and being pushed by circumstance to this remote corner of Ireland. Whatever their origin, the feelings had taken root.

There was no choice but to tread lightly or risk losing her altogether, and on this occasion he chose to let it ride because they would have to leave in the morning, and he didn't want to spoil the mood.

Michael R. Davidson

LONDON

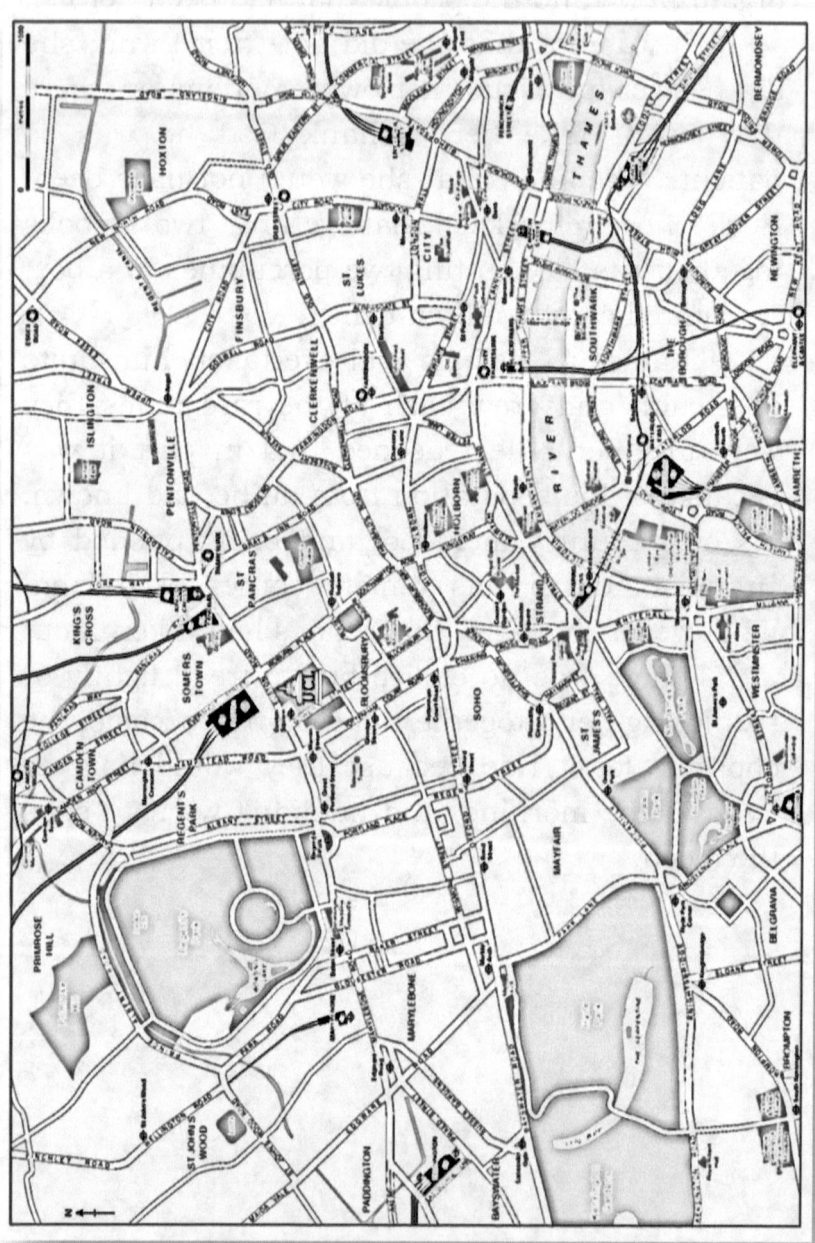

Chapter 3

LONDON

Two days later they waited in a Mossad safe apartment just north of Hyde Park for the arrival of their *bachir,* or senior Mossad officer. They were exhausted from their energetic reunion and the subsequent drive in Sasha's rental from Ireland which accounted for the unusual silence between them as they sipped coffee and waited.

Eitan Ronan was a veteran of the fabled Parachute Brigade, the *T'zanhanim,* and later the *Sayeret Maktal,* the Israeli hostage rescue unit. He was now the head of the Mossad's highly clandestine *Kidon* unit. He was a bear of a man now somewhere between 55 and 60, ten or fifteen years Ramsay's senior, with closely cropped black

Michael R. Davidson

hair sprinkled liberally with gray, and a broad, swarthy face that seldom changed expression. A thoughtful man, befitting his senior status in one of the world's most feared, ruthless and effective intelligence services, he projected a deceptively taciturn, although slightly menacing image. But when goaded into action his response could be swift and savage.

Ronan had been a second father to Sasha since her own father's death, but Ramsay still didn't especially trust or care for the man. He had but one purpose in life – the protection and preservation of the State of Israel. Ewan's relationship with him was an uncomfortable and at times precarious balancing act, considerably complicated by the presence of Sasha in the equation.

The safehouse was a spacious, well-appointed second floor flat in a row house in Bayswater, not far from Notting Hill. Judging from the photographs set in frames around the living room the place was occupied by a middle-aged couple with grown children. The Mossad had innumerable such collaborators around the world willing to contribute in whatever way they could to the preservation of the Jewish state. A discreet phone call with a pre-arranged parole would instruct the occupants to absent themselves for a specified period during which their home would become a temporary locus for espionage.

On this occasion the safehouse keepers had thoughtfully left a tray with a carafe of hot coffee and biscuits on the sideboard in the dining room.

Ronan arrived wearing a baggy suit of some indeterminate dark material, and his white shirt open at the neck revealing a glimpse of curly, iron gray chest hair. His grip as he shook Ramsay's hand and embraced him was evocative of a professional wrestler.

He eyed Sasha, and Ramsay knew he was thinking about their intimate relationship. In the Mossad there were no secrets. If one took a lover, one reported it dutifully. If the bosses didn't like it, you dropped it.

Ronan shed his jacket and tossed it onto the back of the sofa and then engulfed Sasha in his arms and bussed her on the cheek. He grumbled when he discovered there was only one cup of coffee left in the carafe but was instantly mollified when Sasha offered to make some more. He noticed the pile of still untouched biscuits, grunted with anticipation and crammed a couple into his mouth followed by a large swig of lukewarm coffee.

He finally planted his frame in an overstuffed chair and settled into its depths. Still chewing the cookies. "Thank you for coming, Ewan."

Ramsay appreciated the fact that he used his new name, even when they were alone. "What's the job?"

Ronan waited until Sasha returned from the kitchen with a fresh carafe of hot coffee before answering.

"We have an interesting lead to a Lebanese banker here in London who may be acting on behalf of *Voskreseniye*, facilitating illegal arms transactions with Iran."

Ronan stopped talking to pop another couple of biscuits into his mouth and refill his cup from the fresh carafe Sasha had fetched. "I love these things," he said, gesturing at the sweet biscuits. "Where can I get some to take home?"

Sasha looked over at Ramsay and shrugged her shoulders, long accustomed to Ronan's conversational detours, then suggested Marks & Spencer on Oxford Street. "If you can't make it there before you leave, be sure to hit Harrod's at Heathrow International if you pass through Terminal 3."

Ronan solemnly accepted the information as though it were something vital and made an entry in a small notebook that appeared in his paw from somewhere.

Ronan had the notion that these little diversions in the middle of a serious conversations were somehow endearing. Maybe he was trying to ease the tension that stretched tautly between himself and Ewan. Or maybe, Ewan thought, he simply enjoyed pissing people off.

Ronan stopped writing in his little notebook. "Shall we make some plans? The first task goes to Sasha."

Chapter 4

Sasha checked into a modest tourist hotel near Bayswater Road, just north of Hyde Park. It was a good central location, with several near-by tube stations. She used identity documents that showed her to be a German journalist.

A good place to begin any search for information on arms sales is the local "peace at any price group," and there are normally several to be found in any major Western capital. Sasha held them in contempt, but they did have their uses.

It didn't take her long to identify the Coalition Against Weapons Sales, "CAWS" for short, which had its headquarters on a back street near Finsbury Park, north of the city center. It took only a phone call identifying herself as a foreign journalist interested in investigating London based arms dealers to gain an invitation to meet the CAWS director, Anthony Trollope.

She took the Tube from Notting Hill Station via the Central Line, heading east and switched to the Victoria Line at Oxford Circus. Fifteen minutes later she alighted at Finsbury Park and hoofed it the short distance to the CAWS address.

It was a modest suburb with narrow streets lined with shops and lower-end ethnic restaurants. CAWS headquarters turned out to be the rented ground floor of an old manufacturing plant just off the main drag. There was no security at the door, not that she expected any, and once inside she was confronted by a warren of several large dusty rooms around which were ranged tables of various sizes stacked high with papers, and filing cabinets, some with drawers bulging so full that they could not be closed. There was a hot plate on a small table along one wall, dangerously close to the stacks of paper, with a teakettle whistling alongside an assortment of teas, sweeteners, and milk. She counted five people in the place, all engaged in what appeared to be research or typing away at computers. The denizens of CAWS shared a common determined air, and apparently a common predilection for Birkenstocks.

Sasha had chosen to wear unattractive German slacks, flats, and an oversize sweatshirt emblazoned with the Rolling Stones logo. She wore very little make-up, her hair was pulled back into a severe bun, and she completed the light disguise with black rimmed eyeglasses with tinted lenses. The effectiveness of her disguise was confirmed by the fact that men she passed on the street failed to give her a second glance.

Anthony Trollope, 'Tony,' as he preferred to be called turned out to be a fortyish academic type, tall and gangly, with brown hair thinning on top and straggling incongruously down to his shoulders on the sides. He affected a style of dress, perhaps best described as shabby/tweedy. Sasha found him in a small office at the back of the building furiously puffing a hand rolled cigarette while engaged in an animated telephone conversation with someone about arrangements for a demonstration outside Parliament.

Trollope noticed Sasha standing there and waved her distractedly towards a wooden chair in front of his desk. His phone call finished, he turned back to her. "You must be Fraulein Donner. You called earlier?"

"Yes, Mr. Trollope," Sasha used her best German accent. Her native Russian still interfered greatly in her ability to speak accentless English, but she could cover it with the German.

"As I said, I am very interested in writing a piece about arms trafficking in England, and I'm looking into a Lebanese banker named Zakir. I'm sure one of the big papers, perhaps even *Frankfürter Allgemeine Zeitung,* would pick it up. They've published my stuff in the past." She lied easily.

"God, wouldn't we just like to see that bastard go tits up!" said Trollope, his language abilities clearly not on a par with his namesake. "What can we do to help?"

"Well," replied Sasha, "do you have any documents I could look through to give me a start?"

"Of course," Trollope waved his arm magnanimously in the direction of the files, "anything we have is yours, Fraulein. What's your first name anyway, luv?"

"Hilda," replied Sasha, "Hilda Donner."

"Well, Hilda," said Trollope, "Do you see that bit o' fluff over there at that table," he pointed toward a mousy girl studying some papers. "Just ask her to show you what we have, and grab a spare table somewhere. What's ours is yours. You can use the copy machine, too. And a modest contribution to help cover expenses would be appreciated but not required."

The girl's name was Susan Ashcroft, but she told Hilda to call her "Squeaky." Sasha had to work hard to keep from laughing out loud.

"Hallo, Squeaky," said Sasha, "Mr. Trollope said you could steer me to the Zakir files."

"Right over here." Squeaky led Sasha to a file cabinet about halfway along one side wall. Inside were not less than ten file folders filled with press clippings, releases, and photocopies of stray bits of correspondence. She lugged the files over to a table near the teapot, poured herself a cup, and got to work.

Chapter 5

Sasha found Ewan waiting for her in the London safe flat. It was still early afternoon, and this time the safehouse keepers had left an appetizing spread of sandwiches for their clandestine guests.

It was nearing 1:30 PM when she arrived, still in her German disguise, and Ewan was impressed by how effective it was. Nevertheless, her austere German appearance did not prevent him from embracing her as soon as the door was closed.

Laughing, she, slipped out of his grasp and protested, "Ewan! At least let me get rid of these damned glasses!"

"But sweetheart, you make such an attractive little troll! I can't resist you."

"So," she said mischievously, "you think I should keep this look?" She did a playful model's whirl.

He reached around her head and undid the clasp that held her hair. "Don't even think about it."

He kissed her again, but she pulled away quickly. "We can't stand here smooching," She liked this funny American word he had taught her and used it often when they were alone. "Eitan should be here any minute."

"Talk about a troll," grumbled Ewan.

"Now stop that, and play nice when he gets here," she scolded.

Sasha was acutely aware of the animus between the two most important men in her life, and it made her uncomfortable. How could it be that two people who loved her, each for different reasons, could not seem to get along? Her loyalty to Eitan Ronan and the Mossad was unquestionable, but Ewan Ramsay also had earned her loyalty and, altogether to her surprise, her love. Both seemed determined to force her to choose one or the other, and it was a strain to perpetually put off the decision.

She moved to the stack of sandwiches on the dining table. "I'm famished, and we'd better grab a couple of these before Eitan gets here and inhales them all."

In the kitchen, Ewan found a couple of bottles of beer in the refrigerator. As he was returning, the front door opened to be filled by Eitan Ronan's impressive bulk.

Ronan's food radar immediately zeroed in on the snacks, and he headed directly for the table after kissing Sasha on the cheek and tossing a perfunctory greeting in Ewan's direction.

He spread the bread apart to examine the sandwiches' contents, and after sniffing the chicken liver pâté, which he apparently found acceptable, he said, "I've arranged for us to have the apartment until this evening, so we have several hours to review what we know and plan the surveillance." He looked expectantly at Sasha.

She filled them in on the information she had gleaned on Mohammed Zakir from the CAWS files. "They had everything but his address," she concluded.

"I have an idea," said Ewan. He stood and walked over to the telephone stand that stood beside a large leather chair. On the lower shelf was the London Telephone Directory. Ewan opened it. "Let's look him up."

"You're kidding," said Ronan.

Unperturbed, Ewan looked up the "Z's" in the London Metropolitan section. "Obviously, Eitan, the Mossad is not up to date on the latest sophisticated investigative techniques." The simplest solution was more often than not the most effective. *Occam's razor.*

A moment later he could not conceal the triumph in his voice, "Got him! 'Mohammed Zakir, Four West Nine, Maida Vale, West London.'"

Sasha moved to Ewan's side and looked over his shoulder, "That's a fairly high rent district," she said.

MAIDA VALE, LONDON

The area around Mohammed Zakir's residence was upscale with a good deal of pedestrian and vehicular traffic along Maida Vale, a major thoroughfare. Regents Park was a stone's throw away, as well as other tourist attractions, such as Madame Tussaud's Wax Museum and the Sherlock Holmes Museum on Baker Street, and Maida Vale Film Studios. As she admired the neighborhood's splendid Edwardian buildings, Sasha decided she would enjoy spending some time in London as a real tourist. As she chewed on the idea it occurred to her that she had never in her life been a "real" tourist anywhere.

The previous day she had purchased a used motor scooter, a Vespa, in fairly good condition. It fit her requirements perfectly: nondescript, small and maneuverable, but still with decent speed in city traffic. She wore a helmet and a leather jacket with a loose waist to make her profile on the scooter androgynous.

Seated at an outdoor table at a café across the street, she speculated how difficult it might be to break into Zakir's apartment. She guessed that he must enjoy a spectacular view over the rooftops to the park. There was only one vehicular entrance/exit which presumably led to an underground parking garage. It opened directly into Maida Vale as did its pedestrian counterpart closer to the intersection with Clifdon Road. Of course, it was possible that Zakir might slip out through one of the mews surrounding the building. But assuming he was unaware he was being watched, there would be no reason for him to resort to running through other peoples' gardens.

Despite the buds on the trees and the clear sky that promised a warm afternoon, a distinct morning chill permeated the air, and she pulled the leather biker jacket closer around her. She wore her blond hair tucked up under a stocking cap.

It is extremely difficult if not impossible to successfully mount a solo surveillance. In fiction tough private investigators always seem to discover remarkable things on their own, but that

Michael R. Davidson

is just fiction. Sasha's task was to establish baseline information by casing the area of the target's residence, checking entrances and exits, one-way streets, identifying good observation posts, and getting a good "feel" for the way people looked and behaved on the street.

Tel Aviv and Jerusalem were still mulling over the significance of the report on Zakir and the alleged Iranian connection. Operating in London under the noses of a highly competent MI-5 was risky, especially when the target was high profile. Someone like Zakir was certainly known to the British security service. Whether they, too, had reason to surveil him was a thorny question. Her boss, Eitan Ronan, had demanded assistance from Tel-Aviv, electronics specialists, a professional surveillance team, and some highly specialized equipment that could only come via diplomatic pouch. This was not an occasion for flying by the seat of their pants.

After three cups of coffee -- and bad English coffee at that -- she went inside to use the restroom then returned to the scooter where she had chained it to the low, wrought iron fence that enclosed the café's sidewalk tables. She rode a short distance down the street turning left at St. John's Wood Road where she immediately pulled up onto the sidewalk. She stuck the leather jacket and helmet into the scooter's rear compartment. Underneath she was wearing jeans, a light turtleneck sweater, and calf length black leather boots. Pulling a long, woolen jacket from the compartment, she donned it and pulled off the cap, letting her hair fall down her back. Hanging the long strap of a small Longchamps bag over her shoulder completed the change of profile, and she walked back into Maida Vale staying to the sidewalk on the same side of the street as the apartment building. It was nearing nine-thirty A.M.

It was going to be a long day.

Michael R. Davidson

Chapter 6

VYMPEL

In 1981, at the behest of KGB Chief Yuriy Andropov, the Soviet Politburo approved the creation of an elite quasi-military unit within the KGB's Department S. The unit was designated *Spetsgruppa Vympel*, or the Banner Special Group. Its mission was assassination, terror, kidnapping and subversion, especially against the United States and Great Britain. Members of the unit were viewed with awe as "universal soldiers" for whom no mission was too difficult and no task impossible.

Candidates were sent for training to a top secret KGB facility hidden in the northern forests near Kazlu Ruda in Soviet Lithuania. They were instructed in foreign languages and area knowledge in preparation for insertion into their target countries. They were required to achieve a high level of proficiency with a variety of firearms, explosives, and agent handling. Vympel's predecessor unit, *Spetsgruppa A,* had won notoriety by storming the Taj-Bek palace in Kabul in 1979 and killing Afghan Premier Hafizulla Amin.

It was natural that such a unit should be placed under the administration of Department S, the arm of the KGB responsible for "illegals" operations abroad, the elite of the elite of Soviet spies. A *Vympel* member was the supreme illegal. Following the reorganization of Russian intelligence and security, Department S became part of the SVR.

Under the absolute control of General Morozov, the unit had become something more than the executive action department of Russian Intelligence. *Vympel* was now "owned" by *Voskreseniye.*

"Whom will you send," asked Shurgin. "Is anyone already in place in London."

"There are two, but I want our man in Zürich to run the operation."

"Dimov?" Shurgin was skeptical. "After the debacle in Spain,[3] I'm surprised you didn't recall

---

[3] HARRY'S RULES, Michael R. Davidson, 2012

him."

"Don't forget that one of our best men, Drozhdov, disappeared completely on the same operation," he said, "And next to Dimov, Drozhdov was the best *Vympel* had to offer. At least Dimov came back. Zhenya says he is more dedicated than ever, entirely ruthless – a man with something to prove. I like that sort of motivation, and he's still the senior *Vympel* officer I have in Europe. I trust his experience."

"The decision is yours, Yura," Shurgin used the diminutive of his old friend's name. "You know how much I rely on your judgment." He rose and straightened the lapels of his Italian suit. Morozov, whose weight seemed to be increasing with age, envied his friend's still youthful, athletic figure.

Morozov walked Shurgin to the executive elevator, wrapping his heavy arm over the shoulder of his old comrade, a familiarity few others would dare. Access to the 21st floor was restricted to those who carried a key that unlocked this elevator. "I'll prepare coded instructions immediately."

Chapter 7

SURVEILLANCE

The rabbit was on the move, ambling at a comfortable pace south on Edgeware Road in the direction of Marble Arch. Behind him, Sasha was on point, closest to the target, with Eitan Ronan a block behind. Three is not the ideal number for a thorough surveillance operation, but this was only preliminary stuff. A full team would take over once they had established the baseline.

Superb Spring weather had replaced the chill of the previous week. She had left the Vespa in Ewan's care, and Eitan was at the wheel of a rented car about five hundred meters behind her. All three wore concealed radios with wireless earbuds supplied by the London Mossad station.

Michael R. Davidson

Sasha had presented the data they had compiled   last Friday evening over a late pub dinner that had clearly not met with Ramsay's culinary expectations. She smiled at the memory. Ramsay had managed to choke down only half of his meal. Ronan, on the other hand, had inhaled his and then looked inquiringly at Ramsay's plate until the latter had shoved his untouched dessert across the table.

She was pleased by the way her two men, as she thought of them, were getting along. Their common endeavor required teamwork and close collaboration. Wisely, Sasha had declared herself in charge of the surveillance operation thus forestalling any macho head-butting.

Now, as she trailed Zakir, her thoughts were diverted by the quandary in which she found herself – the triangle made up of herself, Ronan, and Ramsay.   Her affections were a point of contention between the two men, each with his particular motivations.

Sasha "owed" Ronan. He had all but adopted her after her father had perished in the 1973 Yom Kippur war -- perished saving the lives of Ronan and his men when he drove his armored personnel carrier between Ronan's unit and incoming enemy rockets. It was in large part due to having someone like Ronan as a role model that she had joined the Mossad. And at thirty-seven, she had convinced herself that she would be satisfied with her "marriage" to the Mossad.

Sasha had resisted her developing feelings for the American. She had argued with herself and with Ramsay that any thought of a permanent relationship was highly improper. They should treat one another accordingly, as fellow professionals, she had insisted.

But Ramsay had persisted, and in the end the barriers she had erected crumbled, perhaps because she had not built them too strongly in the first place, perhaps because she was tired of being lonely, and from their first embrace to the present day her affection for the American had grown and finally metamorphosed into the kind of love she had come to believe impossible.

These thoughts preyed on her mind on a beautiful spring morning in London as she dogged the tracks of the chubby Mohammed Zakir in the direction of Marble Arch. Absent a huge chunk of luck their primitive surveillance operation had little chance of uncovering the alleged Russian agent's clandestine activities.

Their job was to establish a baseline for the subject's daily activities. In time all of this would be turned over to the team of professional watchers, and she, Ronan, and Ramsay would step out of the picture.

Zakir turned left at the bottom of Edgeware Road, heading east now towards Oxford Street, with Marble Arch across the intersection to his right and the incongruous façade of a McDonald's with its golden arches on his left. As Sasha rounded the corner behind him she was just in time to see him again turn left into Great Cumberland Place. The entrance to the venerable Hotel Cumberland was just across the street.

Is he meeting someone in the hotel? We might get a break at last. She transmitted the coordinates to Ramsay as she rounded the corner.

Zakir crossed the street and entered the huge hotel. Fearing to lose him in the large building she rushed inside. As she pushed her way through the doors she spotted him across the lobby at the concierge's desk. He appeared to be asking for information, and after the concierge had spoken a few words in reply, he turned and walked directly back towards her, heading for the doors.

Feeling exposed, Sasha swung abruptly to her right and moved away into the lobby's interior, all the while speaking into the microphone concealed in her sleeve to advise Ramsay and Ronan that one of them would have to take point.

Chapter 8

COUNTER-SURVEILLANCE

Dimov used a Swiss passport to enter the UK. He selected a large hotel in the heart of Mayfair near Green Park. At six in the evening he rode the subway west to emerge at Lancaster Gate, a short walk from The Swan public house on Bayswater Road.

At a table in the rear he met two London-based *Vympel* illegals and outlined a simple plan, the purpose of which was to determine whether Mohammed Zakir was under any kind of hostile surveillance. There is nothing more basic than a counter-surveillance route. The "rabbit," in this case Zakir, would be given a prescribed route to

Michael R. Davidson

follow that took him through a series of checkpoints at which Dimov and his team would be stationed. The goal was to permit the team to spot suspicious activity, such as repeated sightings of people or vehicles that might be following the "rabbit." The route was designed to flush out surveillants by forcing them to pass through the checkpoints.

*****

Across the street in the shadow of Marble Arch Ivan Dimov had been waiting for Zakir's appearance. He wore a baseball cap, tan corduroy slacks, a light green sweater, and a leather bomber jacket. To complete the tourist cover, he carried a single lens reflex camera on a strap around his neck. The camera boasted a powerful zoom lens that Dimov was now directing at the lithe figure of the blond woman who appeared to be following Zakir. She had rushed across the street opposite to enter the hotel after the Lebanese, and now finally had re-emerged. Zakir, in the meantime, had crossed the street again and entered an Indian restaurant where he would have lunch before returning home. Dimov was pleased that the long-time agent was following his instructions precisely.

When he finally focused the lens on the blond woman's face, the Russian's entire body resonated with an electric shock of recognition. He would never forget the woman in Marbella. He snapped several pictures of her and then scanned the street for others who might be following Zakir.

This was a development no one had foreseen. Normally more than a single sighting would be required to confirm surveillance, but this woman was a professional. A decision was required, and Dimov was well aware that *Voskreseniye* wanted this woman very badly.

Nothing could be done today. A snatch would require planning and coordination with Dimov's London-based *Vympel* colleagues. *Best to call off his men now lest they be spotted. Should I risk following the girl?* As much as he wanted to bring her to ground, and as much as he anticipated the feel of his hands around her pretty neck, his training told him that precipitate action was unwise. He could wait.

*****

"We should be watching him at night, you know," said Sasha. It was late, after a long day observing Zakir, and the three were at a pub in central London.

"I agree," mumbled Ronan through hamburger he was devouring. Turning to Ewan, he said, "I don't know what you Americans see in hamburgers. This is just a greasy mess. Look at it. The bread is melting away."

"That thing you're eating has absolutely nothing in common with a real hamburger. It's the sort of thing that gives American cuisine a bad reputation among foreigners." Ewan was pushing some bangers and mash around on his plate without much enthusiasm. "God, I hate pub food. I remember a time when it wasn't too bad, but now ...."

At least the beer was still good.

"So, when will the *memuneh* send the *sayanim* to take over so we can get out of here?"

"Soon. It will be soon," returned Ronan. "In the meantime the job is ours."

"And how are we supposed to do that if we can't even pull off surveillance around the clock?" Sasha was persistent. She didn't like doing things halfway.

"I'll do it," volunteered Ewan. "If anything, the lack of digestible food in London will keep me awake. I'll take the rental car and stake out Maida Vale tonight. You two can take over in the morning."

Chapter 9

TRAP

Sasha and Ronan relieved Ewan at seven thirty the next morning. Fortified with strong coffee from the corner breakfast shop and with reserves of sandwiches packed into the storage compartment of her Vespa, Sasha was prepared for another long day. She hoped their target would do something interesting, something revelatory.

Zakir emerged from his building and Sasha was glad to be on the move, she took up the chase as her quarry ambled at a comfortable pace northward towards the intersection with Hall Road and its beautiful red brick Edwardian buildings. After some fifteen minutes it became clear that he was heading for the Maida Vale tube station, one of the older stations on the Bakerloo line. A subway trip was unpredictable and difficult for their two-man team to follow. They would be separated until their target re-emerged to street level.

"Damn! He's heading underground," she reported to Ronan via her walkie-talkie. "Stand by in the car until we come up for air somewhere, and you can come pick me up wherever it is."

Zakir was already passing under the old station's arched entrance. Locking the Vespa to the metal pedestrian barriers at the curb and grabbing her knapsack, she had to hurry to catch up with him as he disappeared into the station's murky interior.

A man who had been loitering at the tube entrance immediately followed her. As she turned a corner into the tunnel leading down to the tracks she bumped into a second man who held a rolled up newspaper. Intent on catching up with Zakir's receding figure, she did not detect the man approaching rapidly from behind until it was too late. The man she had collided with backed away a step and smiled almost apologetically as he extended the rolled up newspaper toward her. The gesture puzzled her, but before she could react, a chemical spray hit her in the face. She didn't have time to feel surprise before everything went black.

The two men grasped her under the arms and carried her back up the stairs and out to the nearly deserted street where an ambulance now sat idling by the curb.

Dimov was behind the wheel and watched with satisfaction as his accomplices exited the Tube station and bundled Sasha into the rear onto a gurney. As they pulled away from the station, the two men in back changed into EMT uniforms and started to work on Sasha, removing her outer clothing and wrapping her in a sheet before they strapped her to the gurney.

Forty-five minutes later the ambulance pulled into the private jet area of London City Airport where the 'patient' was quickly transferred to a waiting Gulfstream IV that was cleared for a medical transport flight to Zürich.

Chapter 10

ALARM

After his all-night surveillance stint he had gratefully surrendered the vehicle to Ronan and returned to the hotel sorely in need of some shut-eye. Now someone was pounding on his hotel room's door.

The racket did not let up until he opened the door and Ronan pushed past him into the room, clearly in a state of distress. "Get dressed," he shouted. "We don't have any time to waste!"

"What's happened?"

He had never seen the big Israeli so upset, and he immediately intuited the reason.

"Sasha?"

"They took her!" Ronan slammed a fist into the wall. "Right in front of me! We've got to move. *now!*"

The words lanced through his body and gouged deeply into his gut. "What happened?" He grabbed the clothes he had worn the night before and started pulling them on.

"She was on point after the Lebanese and reported he was heading for the Tube. I was too far away to get there immediately, but I arrived in time to see her being loaded into an ambulance. I was too far away to do anything, and taking a shot was out of the question."

Ronan's normal demeanor oscillated between stony tranquility and vigorous determination that bordered on the threatening. Now there was fear in the big man's eyes.

He continued breathlessly. "I trailed the ambulance for over an hour until it finally entered the secure area of the City Airport, and I couldn't follow inside. I watched them load her onto a Gulfstream that immediately took off. I got the tail number. They had her strapped to a stretcher." He paused for a gulp of air. "She wasn't moving."

Sasha was in hostile hands and whatever befell her now, Ronan would always blame himself. He would do so because he considered himself to be omnipotent, and such things did not happen to omnipotent beings. And yet somehow it had.

Ewan wasn't certain that he did not agree, but recriminations would do them no good now. "Ronan," he said as firmly and calmly as he could, "we've got to find out who owns that plane and what flight plan they filed. Then," he continued, "We're going to get a plane of our own and follow. If the Mossad won't authorize it, I'll pay for it myself."

Ronan nodded. "I agree, and don't worry about what the Mossad will do. I'm heading for the Embassy now." With a visible effort, the veteran operative brought himself under control. "You find a charter service – one with jets – and go to the airport and wait for me."

They looked for a brief moment at one another, each fearing that the plane that carried Sasha might escape beyond their reach, especially if it were headed to Moscow.

As soon as Ronan charged out the door, Ewan consulted the telephone directory for charter companies and made several phone calls. Two hours later Ronan joined him at Heathrow.

Thanks to a heads-up phone call from Ronan, he had already given the charter pilot their destination, and a flight plan had been filed. The tail number of the Gulfstream that had carried Sasha away belonged to a plane registered to a Swiss company owned by Yevgeniy Lomonosov. Its flight plan designated Zürich as the destination.

The flight time from London to Zürich would take about one hour, just under five hundred miles. They were painfully aware that by the time their plane had left the ground, the Gulfstream that carried Sasha would already have landed in Zürich over two hours earlier.

"Do you have people in Zürich?"

The Israeli's body sagged in the seat across the aisle from Ewan. "Yes. The jet landed well before anyone could possibly have gotten from Zürich to the airport at Kloten." Kloten International Airport was about 20 miles from the Zürich city center.

"Do they know where she was taken?"

"We're in luck there. We've had Lomonosov's residence under surveillance for some time. If they saw anything unusual, we'll know about it. But that compound is an armed camp. If they have her in there, it will be bloody getting her out."

"Who is Lomonosov?"

Ronan shifted in his seat to look directly at Ewan across the aisle before speaking. "A very bad man."

Kidon operative Michael Mossberg, a tall, lanky man with a shock of jet black hair straying over a high forehead, met them at the airport. He was in charge of a surveillance team assigned to Lomonosov. They drove directly to the building that housed the observation post.

"We're pretty sure they have her in the compound," he said as soon as they were in the underground garage of a large apartment building. "An ambulance arrived at the gates around one P.M. this afternoon. You can imagine that it piqued the team's interest. We wondered who would be taken to the hospital, but the ambulance never left the place. They drove it into the garage, and it didn't come out again. When we learned what had happened in London we figured they must have used the same ruse to get our officer out of the airport here and deliver her to Lomonosov."

Their reception at the observation post on an upper story of a large apartment building was grim. Ewan shook hands all around with the team. There was a lot of technical equipment, including a bulky infrared detection system that was at the moment being assembled. This would allow them to "see through" the walls of Lomonosov's villa. And there was another electronic device he had never seen before.

"What's that," he asked Mossberg.

"A laser listening device. We'll be powering it up shortly."

By now Sasha had been in the compound for several hours, and Ewan didn't want to think about what was happening to her.

The abduction was shocking, not least because it meant that their interest in Mohammed Zakir had been compromised or had been a dangle from the beginning. It could not be coincidence that Sasha had been snatched while surveilling an alleged SVR agent. Did they know she was Mossad?

Mossberg walked to the window and gestured to Ewan. "Come see what we're up against." He offered a pair of binoculars.

Seven stories below and two hundred yards away a blond man with a compact, athletic build stepped out of a car to speak to one of the armed guards at the entrance to a walled compound. His face resolved into sharp focus, and an icicle pierced Ewan's chest. He knew this man.

A large, luxurious villa occupied the center of the compound. The University of Zürich campus lay nearby against the distant backdrop of the *Zürichsee*. Mossberg explained that the villa belonged to Yevgeniy "Zhenya" Lomonosov, a fabulously wealthy Russian "oligarch" according to the stories he himself had placed into circulation. Over thirty percent of Zürich's population was comprised of foreigners, and well-off one's at that, but this Russian stood out. He had set up housekeeping at a grand old property in the city's exclusive District 6. Married, with two children, Lomonosov quickly integrated himself into Zürich's upper stratum crowd. He spent lavishly on everything.

Denizens of the shadowy lower strata, however, knew "Zhenya" Lomonosov a true *vor v zakonye*, a 'thief in the code,' the Russian term for criminal graduates of the *Gulag,* and he had graduated *summa cum laude.* His notoriety made him a person of considerable interest to the Israeli Intelligence Service, not merely because of his criminal activities, but because he was a key player in *Voskreseniye Rossii.*

The organization was an unholy alliance of Russian intelligence and the Russian mafia. At the head of the alliance sat former KGB general Vitaliy Mikhailovich Shurgin, a man whose influence was growing in the Russian Federation.

The blond man Ewan had seen through the binoculars was a *Voskreseniye* operative. More importantly, Ewan could now confirm that he was the same man sent to kill him the previous year.[4] His hand moved involuntarily to the scar where a bullet had dug a deep gash in his side during a shoot-out at a house in Marbella, Spain. The man's name was Dimov, and the worst part was

---

[4] HARRY'S RULES, Michael R. Davidson

that he would recognize Sasha instantly from the Spanish operation. Dimov had a debt to settle with her, and Ewan did not want to think about what form the retribution might take.

Chapter 11

THE MEMUNEH

"We need to get organized around a plan of action." A sense of urgency returned to Ronan's voice.

"We have a couple of ideas," said Mossberg, "but we've been instructed to wait before taking any action."

"Wait?" Ronan was in his face. "Wait for what?"

Mossberg was unruffled. "Eitan, I understand the urgency, but we have our orders."

"Whose orders?" demanded Ronan.

At that moment everyone's attention was arrested by the doorbell - two longs, two shorts.

Mossberg squinted through the peephole, started slightly, and then opened the door and stood back. A man of slight build with a fringe of white hair surrounding a bald pate entered the room. He wore a dark suit with no tie and was alone. Ewan sensed tension in the air as the old man walked into their midst.

He looked inquiringly at Ewan and then at Ronan. The latter said, "Ewan Ramsay, this is David Shalev, the Head of Mossad, the *memuneh*.

Shalev extended a hand.

"Mr. Ramsay," he said in a firm, deep voice, surprising in a man so seemingly frail, "I've heard much about you, and I'm sorry we meet under such terrible circumstances."

The memuneh's hand was dry and delicate, but the returning pressure was firm.

The old man turned to Ronan and said in Hebrew, "You know why I am here, don't you, Eitan?"

Ronan nodded. "Thank you, David," he said, and hugged him. The old man practically disappeared in the powerful, bear-like arms.

The lifting of spirits in the OP was tangible. It appeared that everyone in the room but Ramsay understood what was happening.

Extricating himself with some difficulty from Ronan's embrace, Shalev turned to Ewan.

"Mr. Ramsay, forgive me. I must explain. Shall I call you Ewan?"

Ramsay nodded.

"Good. Please call me David. We are about to undertake a hostile operation with the strong possibility of the use of deadly force on friendly foreign soil. This is not as common as you might imagine, but this operation has as its purpose the rescue of one of our own. Such an action may be carried out ONLY in the presence of the *memuneh*.

"When your colleagues here saw who had come knocking at their door, they realized immediately that we do NOT intend to sit by and merely observe what is happening in that compound over there, hoping that some opportunity to rescue our colleague will present itself." He shot a glance at the window. "No, we will not stand passively by. We will, instead, take pre-emptive action. My personal involvement will lend no physical or operational value to the eventual outcome, but the solidarity of the entire Mossad and the State of Israel are incarnate in my presence. Do you understand?"

Ewan did understand. They were not alone, at the end of a long chain of command, subject to the whims of faceless bureaucrats, lawyers, and timid politicians, as had been the case when he worked for the CIA. Here, at this moment, there was no chain of command. Regardless of outcome they were all one, united and clear of purpose, like a closed fist, by the physically frail but powerful spiritual presence of this old man – the *memuneh*. 'First among equals' he may be, but in this place at this time, they all were equal in their commitment to rescue Sasha.

For the first time Ewan felt a true sense of commonality with the Israelis. He had admired them as if from a distance, and up close had alternately liked and disliked Eitan Ronan, and, yes, loved Sasha. But Ewan had always, even in the old days, operated as a lone wolf, following his own rules. Now he was united with these people by this single purpose, and he knew that he had chosen the right side.

He again grasped Shalev's hand. "Yes," he said, "I do understand. And I'm more grateful than you can imagine."

Shalev regarded him thoughtfully, taking his measure. "Good. Now, gentlemen, shall we devise a plan and start kicking some Russian ass?"

*****

Sasha struggled like an exhausted swimmer up through layers of drug-induced blackness. Her first instinct was to fight, but she was no longer in the London Underground, and the men who had seized her were nowhere to be seen. Instead, as she emerged into full awareness, she discovered that she could not move.

She had no sense of how long she had been unconscious. She forced herself to breathe normally, slowing her heart rate, as she surveyed her surroundings in the dim light. With a shock, she realized she was totally nude, spread-eagled on a metal table, confined by leather restraints at her wrists, ankles, and around her waist and shoulders. For the moment she seemed to be alone in a room that reeked of disinfectant. In her peripheral vision she detected white metal cabinets lining the upper walls.

A door opened somewhere behind her. She heard the click of a switch, and a blinding light mounted on an overhead rack pinned her to the table with an almost physical force. She sensed someone approaching from behind, out of her line of sight. Whoever it was remained still for what seemed like a long time before moving finally to the side of the table.

"We meet again." She squinted against the glare but could make out only the outline of a man who had spoken, a man with blond hair that reflected the bright light.

Sasha squirmed as the man touched her body, caressing her softly with his fingertips. *Control your emotions. Remain calm.*

The after-effects of the drugs rendered the words fuzzy, her mouth as dry as cotton. "Again? Do I know you? I can't see you."

The man laughed softly. There was an intensely cruel edge to the sound, like a knife blade being sharpened. "Don't you recall our encounter in Marbella?"

The two Russians bursting in as she and Ramsay were interrogating a nasty piece of work who controlled secret bank accounts for Voskreseniye. The sharp pistol reports as one of them went down, mortally wounded by Ramsay. And then Ramsay slammed against the wall by a shot from the second intruder. Then this Russian was pointing a gun at Sasha's face uttering imprecations, and that had been his undoing because within a minute he was unconscious on the floor following Sasha's vicious demonstration of Krav Maga, a unique Israeli unarmed combat technique. The Russians had lost a great deal that night, and this one had been left barely alive to tell the tale.

Her eyes must have betrayed recognition. "So," said the blond man, "now you remember."

"Not taking any chances of being beaten to a pulp by a *girl* this time, are you?" she said through gritted teeth.

The man was silent for a moment, and then he showed his teeth in what was more an animal grimace than a smile and waved something shiny before her eyes, too close to focus.

"Do you know what this is?" he asked. "Oh, too close is it?" He moved the object away from her face. "It's a scalpel – a very sharp scalpel. Can you see it all right now? When I come back, I'll help you become better acquainted with it."

He caressed her right nipple with the flat of the blade, and she felt it harden from the cold touch of the steel.

The man laughed and pricked her breast slightly with the point – just enough to draw a small trickle of blood. "I'll see you soon, *dorogaya*, and soon you'll tell me whatever I want to know." He paused, then, "Oh, but I hope you don't talk too quickly. We have a lot of catching up to do."

Chapter 12

Dimov closed the interrogation room door quietly behind him. He was elated. The entrapment operation in London had gone entirely as planned. It would have been better had he achieved the capture of the man, as well, but the opportunity had not presented itself.

Let her wait for a while. In Dimov's experience anticipation of pain magnified the horror of what was to come in the victim's mind. As for himself, the anticipation of separating the soft flesh of the woman with the sharp edge of the scalpel increased his pleasure. And especially *this* woman who had humiliated him. Dimov knew all the pressure points of the human body, the nerve ganglia, and those areas most susceptible to pleasure or pain. *He would play her like a musical instrument. He would compose a masterpiece on her body.*

With an effort, he forced himself out of his reverie and climbed the stairs to the main floor to the study, and the armored doors swung open to admit him.

Zhenya stood by a bank of television screens set into the wall. His attention was on one in particular that showed an image of Sasha strapped to the table in the interrogation room.

"She's beautiful, isn't she?"

Dimov followed Zhenya's gaze to the screen. "For the time being," he said.

Zhenya turned to face Dimov. "I'm afraid you're going to be disappointed, Vanya." He used the diminutive of Dimov's first name. "They want to interrogate her in Moscow. I just received the message. What a shame." He looked again at the nude figure on the screen. "I would have enjoyed participating in this one."

Zhenya Lomonosov, for all his patina of sophistication, was a true *vor* at heart, and Dimov knew precisely what was on the criminal chief's mind. In the world of the *vor v zakonye* women were mere chattel. The first step in 'taming' a woman, or interrogating her, was always rape.

Dimov was indeed sorely disappointed in the orders from Moscow. "I can get a lot more out of her here," he said, "and with no additional risk. Can't you talk to them?"

"They've made up their minds, Vanya. They know the risks of smuggling her out of here and into Russia, but she could be quite valuable to them – to *Voskreseniye*. I'm not going to argue." The needs of *Voskreseniye* took precedence over everything. "The SVR will take over the operation and get her to Moscow via a diplomatic shipment."

Dimov was a soldier, and he knew how to take orders. Discipline had been a part of his life as long as he could remember, and *Spetsnaz* and *Vympel* had provided a welcome and 'acceptable' outlet for his sadistic inclinations. But he *wanted* this woman. The desire he felt to do her harm was overpowering. A thought occurred to him. "They simply want her delivered alive and in condition to answer questions, don't they?"

"What are you thinking, Vanya?"

"Wouldn't it be a good thing if she arrived in Moscow already in a mood to talk? We could still soften her up a bit for the boys in the basement at Lefortovo."

Zhenya didn't answer as he continued to study the woman on the television screen. "We are to turn her over to the local SVR tomorrow. They said it would take a day for them to prepare."

"Yes?" Dimov's question still hung in the air.

Zhenya licked his lips. "How much 'softening up' did you have in mind, Vanya?"

Chapter 13

PLANS

At the window of the observation post a technician worked to focus the infrared beam on the glass of the large picture window of Lomonosov's study. It was tricky because the angle was bad.

Ramsay, Ronan, Mossberg, and Shalev huddled around a table under a halo of undulating blue smoke from Ronan's *Gitane*.

"The compound is heavily guarded," Mossberg was saying. "Besides the serving staff, we've counted twenty muscle boys, all of them armed. They guard the gates and patrol the perimeter like a military unit. And the perimeter is covered by closed circuit cameras."

"A frontal assault was never an option," said Shalev. "We can't go in with guns blazing, not in Switzerland. We would find ourselves surrounded by police and Lomonosov's armed guards immediately, and would face an even more difficult situation that the one we now are in. We have to find another way."

"I agree," said Ronan, "in and out with as little disturbance as possible."

Mossberg had just opened his mouth to speak when the technician who had been adjusting the laser eavesdropping device hurriedly approached the table. The downward turn of his lips told them he carried bad news. "I'm afraid we're running out of time. Lomonosov just said that our officer will be handed over to the local SVR sometime tomorrow. They plan to ship her to Moscow under a diplomatic seal."

Ewan's level of anxiety jerked several notches upward with a physical effect that nearly lifted him off his seat. Before he could speak, Mossberg interjected, "There may be a way."

All eyes turned to the team chief.

"Lomonosov's compound is huge, and it takes a large staff to run it – over 30 people," said Mossberg. "All of those people have to eat. The only food prepared on-site apparently is for the family. We've been watching now for weeks, and we know that every night at nine PM a catering service delivers food for the next day. The service provides prepared food for the maintenance and guard staffs."

Ewan looked at his watch. The time was nearing six PM. Could they move that fast? He studied the *memuneh*. Any chance that Sasha would survive depended on the old man's decision. If she were allowed to fall into SVR hands and sent to Russia, they would never see her again.

David Shalev drummed is fingers on the table. "Given time, we might find a better way, but our extraction team can't get here before tomorrow at the earliest. The transfer of custody to the SVR tomorrow might present an opportunity, but there are too many unknowns. There's no time left." He closed his eyes and for a moment betrayed the fact that he was an old man with a heavy burden. "Michael, we have only a few hours to prepare and execute a plan. Can it be done?"

Ewan held his breath, his heart pounding.

Mossberg said, "The food deliveries are made in a van from the catering service, and normally there is only a driver and a helper. The van should hold three or four in the rear. It's become such a routine that the guards don't check the interior."

"How long does the caterer normally remain in the compound?" asked Shalev.

"From twenty minutes to a half-hour. The van drives straight into the garage under the house. They have to unload it and then retrieve the trays and other empties from the previous night's delivery. There'll be someone from the household staff inside the garage to help, and probably a guard or two."

Ewan knew that twenty minutes inside the target should be more than sufficient if they could discover where they were holding Sasha in time. "We'll have to intercept the van a safe distance away, and we are running out of time to set it up," he said. "Any ideas?"

"We know the route they take," said Mossberg, "and we've been studying ways to get into the compound for some time now. This is our best chance, our only chance."

Shalev nodded. "Make your preparations, Michael, and select the equipment you'll need."

He turned to face Ewan. His face was stern, but when he spoke it was with compassion and the calmness borne of a thousand treacherous operations. "You will want to go in with the team, of course? I want you to know that I do not think it's a good idea. Emotion leads to miscalculation."

Before Ewan could object, Ronan shoved his wide face across the table. "David, with all respect, you know that I also am close to Sasha, and there is nothing in this world that will prevent me from going into that house tonight. Ewan would never say this to you himself, but he has a right to go with us, and I want him with me. I can't think of a better man for this job. It's why I called him here."

Startled at the vehemence of Ronan's words, Ewan closed his mouth and waited, watching the *memuneh.*

Shalev looked slowly from one to the other and sighed. "Very well. But remember, the goal is to get in and out with a minimum of fuss. It is the only way a rescue can succeed. There are at least twenty armed guards in that compound, and you can't afford a pitched battle. Is that understood?"

Chapter 14

GOING IN

Three hours later Ewan and Ronan sat with their backs against the metal sides in the rear of the catering delivery van as it rolled toward their destination. The spring evening had turned cool, and a light breeze rose up the hillside from the *Zürichsee*. Clouds hung over the distant shore promising rain later in the night.

They wore black military style fatigues and each carried a Glock 17 equipped with a silencer and 17-rounds, with extra mags in fitted pouches on the front of their vests. Their faces were covered with balaclavas. Regardless of the requirement to avoid a pitched battle, they knew that it was unavoidable that some measure of violence would be dealt out this night.

In the front, Michael Mossberg, in a catering company uniform, sat next to the driver. The team had decided earlier that it would be too risky to replace the regular catering service driver with one of their own – an unfamiliar face might arouse the guards' suspicion. The driver's assistant, sans uniform, now lay securely bound and gagged on the floor of the van beneath their feet. Mossberg's pistol was jammed into the driver's side.

The three-man penetration squad was optimum for the low profile they needed. Should a face to face gunfight erupt, more men would not prevail. The odds were just too uneven. Nevertheless, in case of such an extreme eventuality, another member of the team was posted at the open window of the observation post, armed with an IMI SR-99 sniper rifle with night sights; its 20-inch barrel, extended several inches by a suppressor, was aimed into the compound. At a last resort, this additional firepower would give them at least a chance if they had to fight their way out.

Each wore a miniature radio transceiver tuned to a masked frequency connected via an induction antenna to tiny ear buds. Darkness had fallen hours earlier, and the streets were nearly devoid of traffic; the staid German Swiss were inside their fine homes in this neighborhood of luxurious villas, just finishing their evening meals and anticipating post-prandial drinks.

David Shalev was the first to spot the lights of the approaching van from the observation post window. It was nine PM. "We see you now," his voice crackled through the ear buds. "There are two guards at the gate, which I am told is normal, and three others patrolling the grounds."

Thermal imaging showed that ten other guards were in their quarters. The whereabouts of the five remaining guards was unknown, as was that of Sasha. The best assumption was that she was being held somewhere in the villa's basement.

"There are five bogeys unaccounted for," Shalev's deep voice was calm over the radio. Be prepared when the van doors are opened inside the garage. *"B'hatzlacha, good luck," he finished.

*****

The driver slowed as they approached the brightly lit gates and the small guardhouse. One of the two guards approached, and the driver waved at him. The shadows cast inside the cab by the bright lights concealed the driver's greenish pallor and trembling hands. Seeing the familiar face, the guard waved the van on, and the gates swung open to admit them.

Ahead, Mossberg watched as a wedge of light spilled out onto the concrete when the garage doors began to roll up. Keeping his pistol jammed tightly into the driver's ribs, he peered into the brightly illuminated interior of the cavernous garage. There was an ambulance parked against the far wall, among several high-end cars. The Russians were probably planning to use the ambulance ruse again to transfer Sasha to the SVR.

Three men waited for the van on the left, nearest the interior double doors that led into the house proper. Mossberg raised his wrist to his mouth and spoke into his microphone to Ramsay and Ronan in the back. "We're entering the garage. There is one member of the household staff and two guards waiting for the delivery. Be ready."

The van entered the garage, and Mossberg prayed that the outer doors would be fully closed before the action started.

The driver swung the van to the right and then backed slowly toward the three people who were waiting by the double doors leading into the subterranean storage rooms of the villa. Mossberg grunted with satisfaction as the garage doors finally dropped completely to the concrete floor, shielding them from the view of the outside guards.

In the rear of the van, Eitan and Ewan readied their weapons as their prisoner on the floor looked on with bulging eyes. They were acutely aware that success, and with it Sasha's life, depended on stealth. No loud disturbance could be permitted that might raise an alarm before they could find her. They had at most 15 to 20 minutes to find her and get back out of the compound.

Mossberg could be of little help at this moment as he had to control the driver, and he could see very little because the truck was now facing away from where the reception group was waiting. Eitan and Ewan tensed, arms extended and pistols pointed toward the van's rear doors.

Chapter 15

When the van's rear double doors were yanked open, Ramsay and Ronan had the advantage both of surprise and the fact that their targets were clearly outlined like silhouette targets on a shooting range by the bright light. The two suppressed Glocks coughed multiple times in unison, and the three men who had gathered at the rear of the van dropped to the concrete. The two leapt out, and Ronan administered a *coup de grace* to one of the guards.

Mossberg forced the driver from the van and bound and gagged him while Ronan and Ramsay dragged the three bodies behind one of the parked cars, where they would not be visible when the outer doors opened again. The driver's eyes were wide with fear as he watched the bodies being dragged away trailing broad, red stripes of blood behind them.

They had discussed whether the team should kill the driver and his assistant in order to eliminate all witnesses, but the killing of innocents was not to anyone's liking, and more practically, they would still need the driver behind the wheel when they left. When these men went to the authorities, as they surely would, it would cause a problem only for Lomonosov who would not willingly confide in the police. The Israelis would be long gone. The only face exposed was Mossberg's, and at that only to the frightened driver, who would be unlikely to remember anything apart from a gun in his ribs.

Seeing the driver's bug-eyed panic, Mossberg put his lips next to the man's ears and whispered. "Don't be afraid. You are safe and will not be harmed – so long as you do as I tell you. Now, sit back and close your eyes until I come back for you."

The driver gratefully squeezed his eyes shut against the images of carnage.

The van had been in the compound less than four minutes. Mossberg stationed himself in the garage to guard the team's rear and ensure control of the escape vehicle. The hardest part of the job lay before the two men now united by their attachment to the woman held prisoner somewhere in the lower level of the villa.

"We're in," Ronan said into the radio. "We're entering the house now." He and Ramsay exchanged silent nods and went through the double doors, weapons at the ready. They encountered no one. A long corridor illuminated at intervals by overhead lights lay before them, bisecting the entire length of the basement with several side corridors. Along one wall just inside the doors were ranged several stainless steel racks containing empty food trays from the catering service. The two crept forward, their rubber-soled footfalls silent against the concrete. Ramsay led the way with Ronan guarding the rear.

Their first task was to clear the area of hostiles, but as they peered around corner after corner into the side corridors no targets presented themselves. The basement was sterile and divided into a series of large rooms used mostly for storage. One side door opened into a refrigerated food locker, and others they tried revealed boxes and crates with unknown contents.

Both were careful to look out for closed circuit television cameras and other security devices, but they saw none. They knew that a series of cameras covered every inch of the villa's exterior and surrounding wall, but Lomonosov apparently believed it unnecessary to wire the house's interior. It took only a few moments for them to traverse the length of the basement to a wide hallway that ran parallel to the back wall. Ramsay heard a murmur of voices that became more distinct as they drew up to the corner.

Two men were speaking softly in Russian, and Ramsay caught the end of a sentence: "...in there for over an hour already."

The second man snickered. "They've been pumping her like dogs in heat!"

On Ramsay's signal, the two stepped quickly into the open. Ronan checked left while Ramsay turned right, toward the two voices. The two guards were about 15 feet away, seated on folding chairs just outside a metal door with a small window in its center. Startled by the intrusion, they looked up from their conversation, their eyes widening with surprise at the black-clad figures, and started to rise to their feet.

Before they were out of their chairs Ramsay dropped them, the 124 grain rounds drilling into their skulls. The two crumpled to the floor without a sound.

There was no one else in the hallway. Opposite the bodies on the floor were stairs leading to the villa's main floor. While Ronan kept watch should anyone come down the stairs, Ramsay rushed to the door. He noted that it was more a metal hatch than a normal door. No sound escaped from whatever was going on inside. He carefully brought his eyes level with the small window.

The sight that met him was at first incomprehensible as his mind struggled to interpret the message his eyes transmitted. He uttered a strangled cry of rage.

Chapter 16

THE TATTOOED MAN

Through the thick glass Ramsay could see what appeared to be a medical facility or first aid station. The walls were lined with neat, white metal cabinets, some with glass fronts that displayed various bottles and jars. The area was brightly, even garishly illuminated by powerful overhead lights.

But what riveted his shocked attention was at the center of the room. His mind momentarily refused to make sense of what he was seeing. A woman was strapped helplessly to a metal table, her legs spread wide and bound to elevated stirrups. He could see rivulets of blood running down her side. She was completely nude, as was the well-built blond man who was vigorously and roughly mounting her from the end of the table, his face frozen in a rictus of sadistic pleasure. Ramsay could see the cords on his neck stand out with each violent thrust of his hips. Standing on the other side of the table was another man wearing a thick, white terrycloth robe that gaped open to reveal a hard body covered with tattoos. The second man was smiling cruelly, observing his companion's exertions as he fondled Sasha's bloodied breast with one hand and held a champagne flute with the other.

Only seconds passed as Ramsay stared transfixed with horror, but it seemed much longer to him. He was uncertain whether Sasha was even conscious, but then she turned her face toward the door, away from the tattooed man. The face that was so dear to Ramsay, the face of the woman who meant more than the world to him, was expressionless, the eyes vacant and unseeing.

Ramsay heedlessly flung open the metal door. He was possessed by a killing rage that propelled him into the room nearly bereft of reason. He didn't want to just shoot these beasts; he wanted to tear them limb from limb. He wanted to taste their blood and watch death empty their eyes. He wanted to be close when it happened.

Michael R. Davidson

The two men jerked their heads up, startled by the intrusion as death entered the room. There was no clear shot for Ramsay to take at the blond man, who was in profile to him and was partially protected by Sasha's raised leg, so his first two shots took the tattooed man full in the chest and staggered him back from the table before he fell, fatally wounded by the frangible bullets that exploded into sharp-edged, organ destroying fragments inside his chest.

An incoherent curse escaped from the blond man. His face was still a travesty of humanity, but he was quick. The Russian backed quickly away from Sasha.

Dimov had known in the instant that he had watched Lomonosov fall mortally wounded to the floor that his own death was only seconds away. He was naked and defenseless before the armed intruder. The blood rage he saw in Ramsay's eyes through the openings in the balaclava was familiar to Dimov, but he did not fear death, and his only thought in that instant was to exact a price for what he knew was coming, something that would be a constant reminder to this woman and the man who had come to rescue her that Ivan Dimov had been on this earth. Before Ramsay could fire again, the Russian ducked behind the metal operating table on which Sasha lay.

As Ramsay rushed heedlessly forward, seeking a clear shot, the Russian grabbed a scalpel from the surgical tray at the side of the table. He stood, his teeth bared, glaring defiance at Ramsay as he raked the sharp blade across Sasha's face, where it sliced deeply through her flesh down to the bone.

Sasha screamed then, even through the fog of her stupor.

Without pausing as he closed the space between them, Ramsay fired. The slug took Dimov in the right shoulder, spinning him away from the table and sending the bloodied scalpel flying against the wall. The frangible round disintegrated in Dimov's shoulder, doing massive damage to bone, cartilage, and muscle. His arm dangling uselessly by his side, he stumbled away from the onrushing Ramsay but tripped over Lomonosov's body and sprawled on the floor, now slippery with the *vor v zakone's* blood.

Ramsay was on him in an instant and rolled him over so the Russian was facing upward. Gouts of blood poured from his destroyed shoulder and he teetered over the brink of unconsciousness. Ramsay slapped him hard across the face, and Dimov's eyes came back into focus.

"No easy way out for you."

Assured that Dimov was aware of what was happening, Ramsay ripped off his balaclava. "I want you to see who I am," he spat into the Russian's face, his voice strangled with rage. "I want to be the last thing you ever see."

Through gritted teeth, Dimov managed to hiss, "*Yob' tvoyu mat'*," fuck your mother.

Still in the grip of his bloodlust, Ramsay withdrew his commando knife from its scabbard on his calf and held it before Dimov's eyes before placing its point just under the Russian's bare rib cage. He slid it with deliberate slowness upwards inside the chest cavity, twisting the blade as it penetrated the lung. Dimov's eyes bulged as the sharp point finally punctured his heart; Ramsay twisted it again and saw death claim the Russian's blue eyes.

Gulping deep breaths to bring himself under control, he stood and turned back to Sasha. He was horrified by the skein of blood that now covered her face. Dimov immediately forgotten, he retrieved the balaclava and pulled it on as he rushed to her and began unfastening the straps that held her down. She made no sound now, and her body was slack in unconsciousness. Ramsay now saw that she was bleeding from several cuts on her torso and breasts, but those wounds were only superficial compared to the damage to her face. The Russian's blade had sliced deeply from her forehead down across her left eye and into her cheek. He could see the gaping lips of the wound on her cheek and the white bone beneath, and he could not see her eye at all beneath the blood that welled in it.

Get her out of here.

He cradled her head and murmured in her ear, "It's Ewan. I'm here. Eitan is here. We're going to get you out."

Her brow furrowed slightly. She was either in deep shock or had been drugged, or both, and he hoped she could not feel the pain. Less than two minutes had passed since he had entered the room.

He spoke into his microphone. "I have her. Is it clear?"

Ronan had remained in the corridor, covering the approach to the room. He now appeared at the open door, taking in the scene at a glance, his eyes pausing when he saw the bloodied torture table.

"We've got to get her out now," rasped Ramsay. "Watch for a minute while I try to find some bandages.

Ronan quickly closed the distance to Sasha and involuntarily uttered a sound between an expletive and a sob when he beheld her face.

Ramsay found some gauze bandages and returned to the table. "I'll take care of this," growled Ronan, "I've seen worse on a dozen battlefields." Ramsay also knew how to field dress wounds, but surrendered the bandages to Ronan. He checked the corridor again.

After a moment, the Israeli said, "OK, I've done as much as can be done here. Let's get her out of here." They found another robe draped over a chair near the table, probably what Dimov had been wearing, and lifted Sasha so they could wrap the garment around her.

Ronan holstered his pistol and swept Sasha into his arms as if she weighed nothing. The expression on his face was unreadable.

Ramsay led the way back through the basement to the garage. They had taken out four guards. Five had been unaccounted for at the inception of the operation.

Alerted by a transmission from Ewan, Mossberg had the rear doors of the van open waiting for them, and they quickly bundled Sasha inside to lay her on the floor beside the bound and still unconscious catering assistant. Mossberg untied the driver and instructed him to start the engine. While Ronan covered the driver from inside the van, Mossberg pressed the button on the wall that controlled the garage doors and leapt into passenger seat.

The van rolled out of the garage.

The two guards emerged from the gatehouse

and stood watching as the van approached. Mossberg instructed the driver to wave at them, but the two men didn't move, and the gate remained closed. The driver slowed the van to a stop.

"What's wrong," asked Ewan from the rear.

Mossberg pressed his transmitter button. "Something's wrong. The guards aren't opening the gate."

Neither Ramsay nor Ronan could see what was going on from the rear of the van. Mossberg's voice crackled over the radio, "They're either waiting for a signal from inside the house or something else is wrong. The gate should already be open. There's no one back there to close the garage door, and that might seem unusual to them. Whatever it is, they've been alerted that something's not right."

"Stand by." David Shalev's voice came over the radio. There was ice in his voice now as his operation appeared on the verge of failure.

The van stood fifteen feet from the closed gates. The driver looked with desperate calf eyes at Mossberg as one of the guards walked toward them, machine pistol at the ready. The second guard remained beside the gatehouse.

The guard stopped in front of the van and pointed his weapon at the windshield. He gestured for the driver and Mossberg to step out.

Shalev saw all of this from the observation post. "Get ready, Michael. We'll take the one at the gate. You take the one nearest the van."

Mossberg opened the passenger side door and stepped out, drawn pistol concealed against his leg. Ronan pressed his weapon into the driver's back from inside. "Don't move!"

As Mossberg cleared the front of the van, Shalev transmitted, "Now!"

Mossberg immediately dropped to his knee and snapped two shots into the nearest guard's chest. Simultaneously, the sniper rifle spat silently from the window of the observation post, and the man standing by the gatehouse was jerked off the ground by the force of the impact. He was dead before his body hit the concrete.

Before Mossberg could take another step the rattle of a machine pistol echoed off the surrounding buildings, and slugs pinged off of the concrete at his side. Every light in the compound flashed on, and somewhere an alarm began to ring loudly. The machine pistol was being fired wildly by a man emerging at a run from the garage. Mossberg instantly realized that this must be the missing fifth guard.

Mossberg dove in front of the van and prepared to return fire, but Shalev's sniper had already put the guard down. They all knew at that point that the time for stealth had passed.

Every guard in the compound would have been alerted and heading for them.

Mossberg sprinted to the gatehouse, leaping over the body of the man he had killed, and pushed the button that opened the gates. As they swung slowly toward the street, Ronan prodded the driver hard in the back and the van moved forward. Mossberg leapt in as they passed through onto the street and sped away.

*****

The night-scopes were rendered useless by the compound's bright lights, and David Shalev had switched to binoculars. He observed the guards converging on the gate area even as a large black automobile shot out of the garage and screeched to a halt by the open gates. Several of the guards clambered into the car preparing to give chase to the escaping catering van.

Shalev gave the order, and the sniper, who had replaced his nightscope with a Nimrod 6x40 telescopic sight, emptied his 25-round magazine into the car's interior, motor compartment, and tires. As the 7.62 rounds slammed into the vehicle, the guards who a moment earlier had rushed to get in developed an even stronger desire to pile out, fleeing to shelter behind the stone wall. Unaware of where the shots were coming from, they could find no target for their own short range weapons to return fire.

With the disabled sedan now blocking the gate, Shalev judged that the van would have no trouble getting away. He ordered his men to pack up all their equipment and sanitize and vacate the observation post as quickly as possible. Shalev intended to be a safe distance away before either the Russians or the local authorities began to comb the surrounding buildings. The rescue operation had not proceeded as he would have preferred, but David Shalev was not a man to abandon his people when they were in trouble, and nor was he a man to regret having done what had to be done.

Chapter 17

ESCAPE AND EVASION

They abandoned the catering service van near where they had first intercepted it. A Mossad medical team consisting of a doctor and a nurse, waited in a sedan. Shalev had brought the medics with him not only to care for Sasha, but as prudence dictated, to be ready in case any of his men should be injured in the operation.

Mossberg took a second car and disappeared into the night. He had a rendezvous to keep with David Shalev.

They left the driver and assistant blindfolded and loosely bound in the back of the abandoned van, knowing they would soon enough break free of the restraints. They would almost certainly contact the Swiss authorities, and Zürich would soon become highly inhospitable.

The surveillance team scattered as soon as they had cleared the observation post and would now take separate routes out of the country. David Shalev, who was travelling on alias documents, would not leave Switzerland until he was certain Sasha was safe.

*****

Sasha had not said a word since the rescue. She sat listlessly between the two medics in the back seat of the sedan as Ronan, with Ramsay beside him, drove out of Zürich to enter the toll road for the one and a half hour drive to Bern. There, they would link up with Shalev and Michael Mossberg, who would be waiting for them at a safehouse. Although it would have been preferable to get Sasha immediately to a fully equipped medical facility, the imperative now was to remain undetected and to put distance between themselves and Zürich.

With the city finally behind them, Ewan turned to the rear of the car and not for the first time asked, "How's she doing, Doctor?"

Dr. Chaim Levy replied, "Her physical wounds are serious, but not life threatening. I'm concerned for her mental state. We can't know anything for certain, of course, until we perform a complete medical examination."

Ewan forced himself through nearly overwhelming emotion to describe what he had seen in the torture chamber.

The doctor nodded. "She appears to be in a near catatonic state, and until we reach the safehouse I won't be able to check for drugs, which I think are likely."

The sight of Sasha on that metal table being ravished by the demented, tattooed Russians replayed itself over and over in Ewan's mind. He knew he would return to that place in his nightmares. Her blank stare as she had turned her face toward him had chilled him to the bone. The Sasha he knew was strong, fearless, and always in control. Perhaps she had been unable to bear her very powerlessness in captivity, the utter loss of control. Would the mental effects of her ordeal be permanent? Would she ever be the same again? He immediately chastised himself. Of course, she would never be the same. Such an experience was indelible. She could never escape the memory or the scars left by the Russian's scalpel. But could she overcome it?

Looking at her now, senseless between the medics, her face swathed in bloody bandages, was like looking at the empty shell of a person, a person robbed of spirit.

Ewan directed his thoughts to a God whose existence he had begun to doubt.

*****

Their destination was not Bern itself, but rather the bucolic village of Wohlen bei Bern, several kilometers west of the city. Shortly after eleven PM Ronan guided the car through the darkened streets to a small chalet on the outskirts. The sky had cleared, and in the moonlight Ewan could see a broad field at the rear and a line of trees in the distance. As the car came to a stop in the drive, a door opened, spilling light onto the front stoop, and the figure of David Shalev strode rapidly out to them, followed closely by Michael Mossberg.

Ewan was instantly out of the car to help Dr. Levy with Sasha, but Ronan already had leapt from the driver's seat and swept her into his arms. The *memuneh* directed them to a comfortable bedroom on the ground floor, and the big Israeli gently laid Sasha on the large feather bed. She was still dressed only in the white terrycloth robe Ewan had wrapped around her during the rescue.

eye for an eye

The doctor and nurse shooed Ewan and Ronan from the room and closed the door. Portable lab equipment and other medical devices were already in position. David Shalev had been well-prepared.

Mossberg had a large pot of strong coffee ready in the kitchen, and Ramsay gratefully accepted a steaming mug. Shalev said, "Michael, I think we all could use some breakfast. There should be some eggs in the fridge, and perhaps some of the excellent local sausage." He spread his arms, and looked at the ceiling. "Good sausage is hard to find in Israel, and I do love it so."

With a slight smile, Mossberg got to work, and soon the aroma of fresh coffee and frying sausage filled the kitchen, and Ramsay discovered to his surprise that he was starving. He couldn't remember the last time he had eaten.

Shalev knew from long experience that different individuals react differently in the aftermath of a dangerous operation, and he had been watching the American closely. In this instance he understood that extreme anxiety for Sasha's well-being, as well as the peril to which they were subjecting themselves had put both Ronan and Ramsay under more than usual stress. He watched now to see how depressurization would affect the American and

103

was gratified to see that he was handling it well. He would strongly have preferred to have taken alive the two men Ramsay had killed in the torture chamber, but it had been his decision to send Ramsay on the mission, and therefore he could hold only himself responsible.

Ramsay didn't bother to conceal his anxiety, but delivering Sasha from the hands of her kidnappers to the safety of Mossad hands had lifted a cold stone from his heart. He realized belatedly that Shalev was speaking to him.

"Ewan, Sasha is in the hands of God and Dr. Levy, and I assure you that I have complete faith in both."

Ramsay nodded. The strong, black coffee and the food did much to revive them all. "Thank you, David. Thank you for everything."

"Duty is duty, Ewan, and our first duty is to one another – our brothers and sisters in arms. There are few enough of us as it is. But now, it's time to consider what to do next."

He wondered what the Swiss authorities would make of the affair.

Chapter 18

EVIDENCE

Chief Inspector Hans Fischer of the Swiss Federal *Bundespolizei* watched the video through to the end. The scene depicted was redolent of sadistic pornography, showing two men taking turns raping and torturing a woman bound helplessly to a metal table. The recording was over an hour long. Suddenly, the attention of the rapists was diverted by a disturbance out of camera range, apparently when the door to the room was opened. The man in the robe, whom Fischer had immediately recognized as Yevgeniy Lomonosov himself, was slammed to the floor by a gunshot to the chest, as the second man, totally naked, ducked behind the table. He was almost immediately disabled by a bullet that ripped through his shoulder. The shooter finally came within the camera's range, a tall, slim figure, dressed in black, face concealed behind a balaclava.

Fischer watched, fascinated, as the intruder leapt onto the wounded man and rolled him over so Fischer could clearly see the Russian's contorted face, but only the back of the attacker's head. The intruder ripped off his balaclava, slapped the Russian sharply, and appeared to say something. The execution that followed was swift and savage. This killing was intensely personal.

Possibly aware of the camera, the intruder replaced his balaclava before Fischer could get more than a partial view of his face, and rushed to release the girl. Another dark-clad, masked figure entered the picture, and the two left quickly with the woman in the second man's arms. Her rescue had obviously been the objective of the raid.

The Chief Inspector could find within himself no compassion for the two dead men whose bodies still lay in a pool of gore on the tiled floor of that abominable room in the villa's basement. Both were villains of the basest order – clearly demonstrated by the atrocity shown on the video. He harbored no doubt that the rescue operation had been the work of professionals. A man like Lomonosov, he reflected, made many enemies, and deservedly so.

Getting into this room, the *vor v zakonye's* inner sanctum, had not been easy. Alerted by frantic calls from neighbors reporting multiple gunshots from the compound, local police units had converged on the residence. The first responders had been met at the gate, blocked by a Mercedes sedan riddled with bullet holes, by a group of armed men, none of whom spoke either German or French, and a tense stand-off had ensued. The men denied entrance to the compound, and they threatened the uniformed police officers with machine pistols.

Fischer had been notified immediately of trouble at the Lomonosov residence, even before the uniformed officers had arrived on the scene and had immediately ordered a helicopter to take him from Bern to Zürich. The Inspector was always notified of anything that concerned Lomonosov because he was in charge of the investigation BUPO had launched against the Russian Mafioso soon after he turned up in Switzerland. The infamous Zhenya was well known to the Swiss authorities, but they had been unable to pin anything on him. The man had an uncanny ability to deflect any effort to penetrate his operations.

The Chief Inspector was painfully aware

Michael R. Davidson

that the Russian's money could and had corrupted his own investigation. But this night was different. Given the fact that shots had undeniably been fired, the physical evidence of a bullet-riddled automobile, not to mention the two bodies that had been spotted immediately by the uniformed police just inside the gates to the compound, there was nothing on earth that could have prevented Fischer from entering the compound that night.

He had summoned the BUPO SWAT team, the Einsatzgruppe TIGRIS, complete with helicopter gunship support and had arrived at the compound gates himself, backed by an armored personnel carrier armed with a 50 caliber machine gun. Devoid of leadership and faced with this firepower, the compound guards had quickly discovered a heretofore unknown docility. All were now cooling their heels behind bars at Zürich police headquarters. He would question them later.

Fischer strode through the gates imbued with a sense of long delayed victory, like a long distance runner who had passed his rival just before the finish line. He had dead bodies, witnesses who would testify that weapons had been fired, the destroyed sedan. He declared the entire compound to be a crime scene. No Lomonosov attorney could now prevent his entry, and no bribed official could now forestall his investigation.

Following the trail of corpses, two at the gates, one in the drive, and three more inside the garage, the SWAT team had cleared the house, room by room. They had quickly discovered the bodies of Lomonosov and Dimov.

Lomonosov's distraught wife and their two children were now sequestered in the living room of the huge villa. The household staff was held in another part of the house and would be questioned later.

It had taken a team with a battering ram to penetrate into Lomonosov's study, and when he entered through the destroyed armored doors, the Chief Inspector's attention was attracted immediately by the glowing television monitors that occupied an entire section of wall of the richly furnished room. There were several small monitors showing black and white images of the compound's perimeter, but a larger color screen displayed the carnage in the torture chamber where his criminal scene investigators going about their tasks. Lomonosov had apparently been fond of watching what took place there.

Beneath the color monitor was a video recorder and a shelf of VHS cassettes. He had rewound the tape in the recorder and played it back to discover the brutalization of the woman

Michael R. Davidson

and her rescue. Fischer shuddered to think what the other cassettes might contain.

The violent events of this night freed the Chief Inspector to rummage through the villa at his leisure. He had suffered through over a year of frustrated investigation and dead-ends. Lomonosov had been like a master prestidigitator whose audience knew they were being fooled but was unable to discern the means. The villa should yield a bonanza of evidence that the Chief Inspector confidently anticipated would break open the Lomonosov criminal ring. There were months, perhaps years of work ahead. And from what he already had seen there was a strong likelihood that certain intelligence services also would be interested.

He silently thanked whoever had mounted the raid. It had been well-organized and executed with precision. Two employees of a local catering company that serviced the villa had breathlessly reported that they had been kidnapped and forced to participate in the raid. One of them had witnessed the killings inside the garage, as well as the gun battle at the gates.

Fischer reasoned that at least four people had mounted the action – three actually penetrating the compound and a fourth positioned near-by with a rifle. His men were now searching for the vantage point that had been used by the sniper. As yet there was no trace of the raiders. Fischer doubted that they would ever be identified. *And he didn't particularly care.*

Chapter 19

Wohlen bei Bern

Over an hour passed before Dr. Levy emerged from Sasha's sickroom. At the sound of the opening door, all four of the waiting men hurried out of the kitchen to confront him.

"The blood work shows a considerable amount of cocaine in her system," he began, "but the drug has been combined with something else that I cannot identify. I think we are dealing with a sort of drug-induced psychosis, a state normally associated with chronic drug use."

Ewan started to speak, but Shalev waved him to silence. "Please continue, Doctor."

"As I was saying, although such psychoses are associated normally with chronic drug use – amphetamines, cannabis, ecstasy, cocaine – this appears to have been caused by an injection of a cocaine-based substance I've not seen before. She could well be suffering hallucinations, as well as some memory loss and confusion. Once the drug has been eliminated from her system, we should begin to see some improvement. But I'm worried by the exotic nature of whatever it was she was given." The doctor paused because he knew that the information he had now to impart would be disturbing. "As for the wound to her face, I'm sorry to have to tell you that the scalpel destroyed her left eye. It cannot be restored, and I've removed the eye."

Ramsay sat down, shocked and dismayed despite having feared this very result from the terrible wound Dimov had inflicted. He covered his face with his hands. Ronan moved to his side and placed a surprisingly gentle hand on his shoulder.

"Ewan, she'll pull through this. She's strong, stronger even than we might believe." Working hard to control his own voice, he added, "With your help she'll get over this."

Dr. Levy continued his clinical but nevertheless horrifying description of Sasha's condition, "There is considerable vaginal tearing, of course, but that will heal completely. Of more concern is the fact that she is still unresponsive to verbal stimuli." Levy flopped wearily into a chair.

"As soon as we're certain the drugs have worked their way out of her system, we'll administer a tranquilizer that will allow her to sleep. That will do her some good, but she will remain psychologically vulnerable for some time as her mind sorts out what was done to her. I can't predict how long that will take or what the lasting effects may be. We can begin treating the physical trauma here, but she will require hospitalization for ... reconstructive surgery and rehabilitation. What I can tell you is that she should not be moved for some time, perhaps a week. The best medicine for now will be rest and tranquility. My assistant and I will, of course, remain with her."

Ewan's throat constricted. Something was breaking inside his chest and he struggled to hold it together.

The room was silent as they absorbed the doctor's report. Finally, David Shalev spoke. "The chalet is rented for two months and appears to be a secure place for the recuperation Doctor Levy recommends." The sun was rising behind the trees that bordered the backyard of the house. Glancing out the window at the growing light, he continued, "I'll remain through the day, but I must return to Tel-Aviv. Tonight I'll be on a train back to Rome to catch a flight tomorrow. Michael, I would like you to remain her with medical team to provide security."

"When the drugs have worn off, she may relive the brutalization to which she was subjected, and rape victims are prone to feelings of guilt, however irrational," said the doctor. "I have learned that you have a special relationship with the patient, Mr. Ramsay. Your presence during that period could be either beneficial or detrimental to her recovery. We can't be certain."

Could it have been only two days ago that Sasha had been abducted in London? Ewan's sense of time was completely distorted. Ragged did not begin to describe his current state.

"Thank you, Doctor Levy. I think you should return to your patient now." Shalev dismissed the doctor. "Ewan, we need to make some decisions."

When Levy was out of the room Shalev said, "Although the circumstances that brought us together here are extremely unfortunate, there may be a silver lining."

The *memuneh*, who had taken the chair next to Ramsay, put a hand on his knee. "Ewan, what happened to Sasha was an atrocity. None would deny it. But I suspect that her *rescue* will yield considerable benefit. We had to evacuate Zürich because the Swiss authorities will by now be swarming all over that compound. The events of last night are sure to have repercussions well beyond a simple criminal investigation. We know that the Swiss were extremely concerned by Lomonosov's presence in their country and what he might be doing here. Most importantly, we *know* that Lomonosov was intimately involved with *Voskreseniye* and the SVR. Consider for a moment what the Swiss might discover in that villa. I would give a great deal right now to be standing in the shoes of whoever is in charge of the investigation."

Ronan rumbled his agreement. "This will do severe damage to their organization."

Shalev nodded, "Yes, it no doubt will. By kidnapping our officer they inadvertently brought disaster and ruin upon themselves. And there is something more. We have even more confirmation of the SVR's direct involvement with *Voskreseniye*. Perhaps there is no difference between them, at all."

Despite his aching concern for Sasha, Ramsay was intrigued by the potential ramifications of the *memuneh's* speculation. "If the Swiss make this public it'll blow the lid off of *Voskreseniye*."

"Not to mention the damage it will do to the SVR and the Russian government," said Shalev. "We can only hope at this point, but if information does begin to trickle out of the Swiss investigation, I will see to it that our Station in

Switzerland 'volunteers' some modest leads that might help it along. We must exercise caution to conceal our role, of course."

Michael R. Davidson

Chapter 20

REPERCUSSIONS

If gunfire in Zürich was a rare event, an all-out battle in the staid city's most prestigious residential quarter was completely unheard-of. The first press reports of the events at the Lomonosov compound were fairly straightforward. There were eyewitness accounts from neighbors, and an enterprising reporter managed to track down the catering service employees who had been at the center of the action. The story ran under banner headlines in all the Swiss papers.

Yevgeniy Lomonosov had cut a wide swath through Zürich society despite his unsavory past, a fact many people had chosen to overlook in a city where money speaks loudly. His Swiss acquaintances had chosen to adopt a "romantic" view of the Russian as a sort of reformed pirate. But as the truth began to leak out, those same people expressed shock and indignation that such a person would have been allowed into Switzerland in the first place.

Chief Inspector Fischer basked in the spotlight. As the head of the investigation he was much sought after by the media, and after several television appearances he found that he enjoyed the attention and the novelty of being recognized on the street.

The extent of illegal activities revealed in Lomonosov's files was staggering. It would take years to untangle the web of front companies, banks, and corporations that made up his criminal empire. Fischer realized he could live off of this case for the rest of his life. He would retire and write a book when it was over.

Even more intriguing was the thread of evidence the Chief Inspector had discovered of a link between the Russian Intelligence Service and Lomonosov. That a criminal organization like the *Bratsvo* would be acting in concert with the official Russian establishment was heretofore unsuspected. It explained how Lomonosov had been able to operate so much more effectively than even the vaunted Italian Mafia.

When the evidence was presented to the

Michael R. Davidson

Swiss Government, the first official action was to expel nearly every Russian diplomat from the country. This excited worldwide press attention, and the Lomonosov – SVR connection became an international *cause célèbre*.

In Moscow a search for scapegoats began in earnest.

*****

For once Vitaliy Mikhailovich Shurgin was not meeting his old comrade, General Morozov, in the latter's office at SVR Headquarters. Instead, he had chosen a more discreet rendezvous in a safehouse in central Moscow. The SVR was in an uproar over the Zürich mess which had deeply embarrassed the Yeltsin government. Yevgeniy "Zhenya" Lomonosov and the *Bratsvo* were well known in Moscow, and the newly unrestrained Russian press was having a field day. The embattled Yeltsin government was reeling from the storm of condemnation that was raging around the world and as yet had no idea what it was about. The new Russian political class around Yeltsin was as yet but dimly aware of *Voskreseniye* activities – activities that, after all, were calculated to bring about their downfall. Shurgin realized that heads would roll, and he was determined that one of them would not be his.

General Morozov did not look well when he entered the apartment. Dressed in mufti today, the normally robust man had obviously lost weight. His deeply lined face betrayed lack of sleep.

"*Gospodi*, good Lord, Vitya," he said in a voice laden with weariness, "I could never imagine such a thing. The Forest[5] is on tenterhooks. Everyone is walking around on egg shells, looking over their shoulders. Primakov is on the warpath searching for scapegoats."

Primakov, who was a special favorite of Yeltsin, had been appointed to his post in 1991. Though a veteran KGB operative, Primakov was out of the *Voskreseniye* loop due to his connection with Yeltsin.

Shurgin knew and disliked Primakov. A long-time and influential member of the Soviet intelligence establishment, Primakov was an Arabist, and had served as Yeltsin's special envoy to Saddam Hussein after the first Gulf War. He wanted to steer Russian intelligence activities away from traditional "Cold War" objectives and had drastically reduced the number of SVR

---

[5] SVR Headquarters at Yasenevo

personnel, closing SVR *rezidenturas* in Latin America and Africa.

Shurgin, in contrast, still considered the United States to be Russia's *"glavniy vrag,"* the main enemy.

Shurgin had to guarantee somehow that what was left of *Voskreseniye* would survive the internal investigations and purges sure to be launched by Yeltsin and Primakov. Without his network of collaborators within the Russian intelligence establishment, Shurgin's plans to one day rule Russia would be jeopardized, but Morozov's control of the widespread *Voskreseniye* network within the SVR was absolute. And even without the SVR organization Shurgin might be able to retain his power base in Russian industry, leaving him still a force to be reckoned with.

"What do you think, Yura. Can we limit the damage?"

Morozov flopped heavily into a chair. "It won't be easy. I think he realizes he is powerless against me personally," he meant Primakov, "but I can feel their breath hot on the back of my neck, and there will be casualties. Primakov's people have begun to sniff around in Directorate 'S', but he fears me. Our management of weapons systems sales to Iran and the covert assistance we provide to Iran's nuclear weapons program are too important."

"In retrospect, it was, perhaps, a mistake to put Dimov in charge of the London operation. You already had two men in place there."

Shurgin was careful to modulate his tone, but he sensed that his words sent a chill of alarm down Morozov's spine. The two were longtime friends bound to one another by the secrets they shared. They had plotted together to create *Voskreseniye*, had reveled in its early successes. Shurgin relied on Morozov more than any other throughout the long slog from Soviet collapse to *Voskreseniye* success. But Morozov knew too much about Shurgin's less savory activities. *Could there be danger from this quarter?*

"You were with me when we made that decision, Vitya," said Morozov. "You agreed that Dimov was the best man for the job because he might recognize the operatives from Marbella."

Shurgin banished expression from his face.

"I relied on your judgment, Yura. Dimov was too close to your pet, Lomonosov. Inserting him into London was a risk. It crossed operational boundaries."

Despite the overwhelming burden of the Primakov investigation, Morozov was clearly stung by Shurgin's words.

"As I said, Vitya, you agreed to the plan. And you must admit that had Dimov not been in London, we would not have discovered who was operating against us. Only he would have recognized the woman from Marbella."

Dimov's report that he had recognized a member of the team that had done such serious damage to *Voskreseniye* the previous year had seemed fully to justify the London operation. Shurgin had been excited and motivated by revenge no less than Dimov.

"And what if the Iranian operation has been compromised?" Morozov considered the worst outcome.

"Primakov is well aware of the operation with the Iranians."

"Yes," said Morozov, "but he doesn't know how deeply we personally are involved, or how much money we're skimming from the weapons sales, and he knows very little of *Voskreseniye*. He hoped to clip our wings by cutting back SVR personnel and *rezidenturas*."

Morozov rubbed his eyes wearily and softened his tone. "We can survive this, Vitya, but not without," he searched for the right word, "discomfort. Even from the Western press accounts it's clear that Lomonosov's organization and activities on our behalf, our use of SVR channels to support him, have been compromised. We're in for some rough sledding, especially as more details become public."

Shurgin did not like what he saw when he looked at Morozov. The man was like an egg with a cracked shell, ready to break wide open. They were the same age, but the SVR General looked 10 years older. The weight of the General's alarm and pessimism was dragging him ever more deeply into a pit of depression, and that could be dangerous. He had always been the more cautious of the two old comrades, the calm one who tempered Shurgin's inspired but sometimes reckless ambition. Where once there had been unquestioning loyalty and strength Shurgin now detected a *soupçon* of weakness.

"The situation is precarious." Shurgin said. *He needed to reassure Morozov.* "But we will come through this, old friend, you'll see. We must keep our eyes on the goal. It won't be too much longer before we finally control this country from top to bottom."

Morozov shook his head mournfully. "You are ever the optimist, my friend. I admire this in you, but realistically the damage to our SVR operations will be catastrophic."

"Realistically, we must try to control events and limit the damage," Shurgin interrupted him. "You should return to The Forest so you can stay abreast of where Primakov's people are poking their heads."

Michael R. Davidson

Shurgin rose to his feet and put an arm around Morozov's broad shoulders. "Go on, now," he said gently, "and I'll do all I can from my end."

"I never thought the day would come when I would fear walking into my own office," said Morozov.

Chapter 21

It was three days before anyone besides Dr. Levy and the nurse, Dahlia, was permitted into Sasha's sickroom. Ewan assumed that Ronan would accompany him, but the Israeli gripped him by the shoulder and said, "I think you should go in first and alone."

Ewan was both surprised and grateful at the big Israeli's unexpected sensitivity.

Sasha was propped up in the bed with several large pillows behind her, dressed in a blue silk robe. The left side of her face was almost completely covered with a surgical dressing and she'd combed her long hair so that it at least partially covered the bandages.

She gave him a wan smile. "Ewan. They told me you were coming." Her voice was almost inaudible at first. Then, more strongly, "I know I look awful." She put a hand to her face.

A wave of emotion swept over him seeing her like this, so helpless and wounded. She had lost weight and looked so fragile that he was almost afraid to touch her.

"What," she said softly, "no smooch?"

He hesitated only for a second. When their lips met, he could sense her frailty, and did not linger. He stroked her hair and put his mouth close to her ear, catching the scent of strawberries from her hair.

"Welcome back," he murmured. "I've missed you."

He sat on the edge of the bed and took her hand.

Turning the bandaged side of her face away, she said, "I don't remember very much. Images and recollections seem to slip into my brain and out again. It's my fault, really, the way they trapped me in London."

"It's absolutely *not* your fault. Not even Eitan saw that coming. It was a trap from the beginning."

She ignored him as she tried to concentrate her thoughts. "I remember waking in a room that smelled funny. I couldn't move. And that Russian from Marbella was there. Then there were two men ..."

Her voice trailed away, and he hoped that whatever drug the Russians had used would leave a void in her memory.

"You mustn't think about it. We're together now, and I don't intend to let you out of my sight again."

She put a hand to the bandages. "The doctor said I lost my eye." Her voice was far away. "I'll have to wear an eye patch, like a pirate."

The attempt at humor was a good sign.

"I happen to admire pirates, especially pretty blond ones. We'll take it a day at a time, just a day at a time. And we'll be OK. The doctor says you're recovering nicely."

"I know I'm supposed to be a tough Mossad operative," she said, "but it's so hard."

Another tear trickled down her right cheek, and Ewan feared that his presence was not helping things. Yet he could not tear himself away.

He was saved by the nurse. "I think that's enough time for the moment, Mr. Ramsay. She needs to rest awhile now."

He leant and kissed her cheek, tasting the salt from her tears. "You're as tough as they come."

She squeezed his hand.

*****

Ronan stood when Ewan returned to the living room, his eyes questioning, but it was a moment before Ewan could control his voice enough to speak. "She's going to need a lot of support, Eitan."

The Israeli said, "She has a lot of support. She has you, and she has me, and she has the Mossad. Don't underestimate how strong that girl is."

"She's not feeling so strong right now."

The doctor had followed the nurse into Sasha's room, and when he came back out the two collared him for a conference.

"Her eye, as I said, could not be saved. I expect her to be able to travel within a week, and we will get her back home where she can be more properly treated, including plastic surgery to repair the damage to her face. The cut was deep but clean, made with a scalpel, and so I hope there will be only minor permanent scarring. It's healing nicely, but the cosmetic boys at the hospital will be better able to minimize it. Once we get her back to Israel, I estimate she will need another week, if not longer, in hospital. Then she will require rest, a lot of it."

"Is there a plan to get her to Israel?" asked Ewan.

"Michael Mossberg joined the group. "We're working on it now. Nothing very elaborate, but the key is to get out of Switzerland undetected. There's still a lot of interest in finding the people involved in the Zürich affair. We plan to drive into Italy, probably all the way to Rome, and get her on a plane there. We'll paper her as an Israeli citizen who was in an automobile accident. The doctor and nurse will travel with her. Frankly, the sooner we all get out of here, the better, and that goes double for you two desperados," he finished, looking at Ramsay and Ronan.

"I'm going to Israel, too," said Ewan.

Mossberg looked at Ronan for confirmation.

Ronan thought for a moment. "We'll have to get alias documents for him," he said to Mossberg. "I think you can leave and take care of that now that we're here, and you're right: it's high time we all got out of the country. Tell them Ramsay and I will pick up our documents in Paris. We can't all fly out of Rome together, and given her condition, Sasha will be quite visible. We don't know how much of a description, if any, the authorities have of her.

Chapter 22

Chief Inspector Hans Fischer sat in his office at Number 29 Nussbaumstrasse in Bern. He was deeply engrossed in a printed report that his secretary had just placed before him.

There was no way to confirm that the subject of the report was the same woman he had watched being tortured and raped in the video and thus he could not order that she be detained. But her destination was interesting.

A little over two weeks had passed since the events in Zürich, but the time had passed with amazing rapidity for the Chief Inspector. He had become a media star, a status which did not discomfit him in the least. There was a steady stream of interview requests, and lately he was not so subtly scouted by one of the major political parties as a potential candidate for a seat in the Federal Assembly.

The message he was reading was from the Italian police via Interpol. Fischer had kept what he had observed on the video tape of the rescue strictly secret. The woman was the only lead he had to whoever had attacked the Lomonosov compound. These were extremely professional people, and the Chief Inspector did not want to them to realize that he had a lead. In all likelihood they already were out of the country, but the woman's injuries had looked serious on the tape, and a badly wounded woman was not so easy to move or conceal.

Fischer had alerted Interpol that he was interested in a woman with a serious injury to her face, who may be travelling. That alert had gone out the day after the events at the Lomonosov compound, but there had been no leads. Now the Italians reported that a woman matching the description, accompanied by a doctor and a nurse had boarded an El Al flight from Rome to Tel Aviv that same morning.

His inability to positively identify or detain the woman was not, in the Chief Inspector's personal opinion, entirely negative. In fact, Fischer was secretly grateful to whoever had attacked the compound. Had it not been for them, he would never have gotten inside.

If it had indeed been an Israeli team that killed Lomonosov, Fischer did not want the

Michael R. Davidson

complications that inevitably would follow if it were to become public knowledge and part of the investigation -- better for his purposes that the identities of the attackers remain a mystery so he could concentrate his energy on Lomonosov's criminal activities, a much more fruitful line of inquiry. International complications that could detract from the criminal investigation were best avoided. Most of the public and half of the police were convinced it had been the work of a rival Russian gang.

A team of forensic analysts, many of them with financial backgrounds, had been assigned to him, and they were poring over the documents and computers recovered from the compound. Electronics experts were studying the interesting unmarked satellite communications electronics and other unusually sophisticated equipment discovered in Lomonosov's secret study, and a team of codebreakers was working on the many encrypted documents that had been unearthed.

Fischer was still processing the unexpected visit a few days earlier from a representative of the Russian Government. When the request for an audience had been received he was predisposed to expect a plea for discretion in revealing the results of the "Zhenya" investigation, as it had become known in the press. He was therefore surprised by what his visitor had to say.

Anatoliy Gradasov had introduced himself as a personal envoy of none other than the President of the Russian Federation.

"Only three people are aware of my instructions," he had begun, "and now, counting you, there are four. I have come to you with a personal request from President Yeltsin, and I beg you, no matter what you decide, to treat it with the utmost discretion. Lives are literally at stake."

Fischer steepled his fingers as he studied the man. The Chief Inspector was somewhat nonplussed by Gradasov's opening gambit. *What is this bugger up to?*

To Fischer's eyes, the Russian was the archetypical "little gray man." He was somberly dressed and well-groomed (for a Russian, he thought), thin, about 45 years old, with a widow's peak of black hair lightly sprinkled with gray. *He looks like a bookkeeper.*

"I'm listening."

"The President is in a precarious position," Gradasov began. "He is beset from within and without by a deteriorating economy, a restless population, criminal gangs that operate with impunity, and some very dangerous enemies – enemies not only of the President, but of our new Russian democracy, as well. Powerful forces are at work to return Russia to the old ways, to destroy the work the President has done to bring our country out of the darkness of dictatorship and repression."

Fischer nodded, continuing to watch Gradadov suspiciously. "All of this is well-known. The situation in your country is deplorable."

"Yes," the Russian shook his head as if he had trouble believing the enormous problems faced by his country. "But – this is the reason I was sent to see you – not everything that is happening is the result of merely random events. The wealth of Russia is being concentrated into a very few hands, and even the so-called oligarchs often front for others, so that it is impossible to determine who owns what. There is a pattern, a secret hand behind much of what is happening. We have heard only whispers of a revanchist group dedicated to the destruction of democracy, but until now we've been unable to penetrate the secrecy that surrounds and protects it."

It was Gradasov's turn to study the Chief Inspector, and the Russian smiled thinly. Fischer had not missed the import of the words 'until now.'

Fischer's mind was racing. He had a glimmer of where his visitor was going with this story, and the implications could be enormous.

"Are you claiming that the Zürich affair is somehow related to this 'secret group'?"

Gradasov mentally parsed his words before

enunciating them. The conversation had arrived at the frontier of dangerous territory. The President had given him *carte blanche* to say whatever was required to convince the Swiss, but that was typical of Yeltsin, a man who vacillated between extremes of emotion, especially in these days of growing chaos. And his drinking had become worse of late. Now Gradasov had to decide what to reveal and what to conceal, and he felt the weight of the responsibility. Fischer was an intelligent man and a careful, patient investigator, but the Zürich affair had obviously opened new vistas for him. Gradasov suspected that ambition born of newly found celebrity was now driving the Chief Inspector at least as much as his professional duty. Fischer would do nothing to jeopardize his own position, and so, Gradasov reasoned, he could be trusted not to go to extremes.

"We have long suspected that these people have heavily infiltrated the SVR and that in some way they also are involved in criminal activities. What you have uncovered of Lomonosov's affairs and the hints you seem to have found of a linkage between him and the SVR alarmed the President. The publicity the case has provoked has served to damage and weaken the government when in reality the culprits are *outside* the government and working actively against it. So in a perverse way, your investigation is aiding the culprits, and giving ammunition to the President's enemies in the Supreme Soviet and the Congress of People's Deputies." He referred to the growing tensions arising from disagreements over Yelstin's reform policies. Earlier in the year there had been a move to impeach the President.

Fischer was not so easily persuaded. Gradasov's mission could well be a Russian ploy to deflect attention in favor of a bizarre conspiracy theory. He believed he had solid evidence of SVR involvement with Lomonosov. How could this be possible if the Russian government itself were not a party to it?

The perceptive Gradasov responded to Fischer's unspoken suspicion. "Chief Inspector, I shall not propose anything that could inhibit your investigation. The damage already has been done to my country's international prestige and credibility. It is too late to assuage such widespread suspicion, and we will just have to live with it. But we do have a request to which we pray that you will accede."

Fischer was very alert now. The Russians were clever, and he was wary of traps. "I'm listening."

Gradasov sighed. "You are rightly suspicious, Chief Inspector, as I would be, but you must realize that you are in the superior position. We can only beg your indulgence and hope for a measure of cooperation."

"Cooperation?" *Now we're getting to the crux of the matter.*

"We understand that you have in your hands a great deal of information on the inner workings of the Lomonosov organization, which is known in Moscow as the *'Bratsvo.'* Your investigation must make them very nervous. We ask only one thing of you, Chief Inspector: that you share with us on a strictly confidential basis, any information that you might come across that can tell us about this secret group, perhaps allow us to identify its leaders. We are in peril, sir, not only the Yeltsin government, but our country, as well. Our most secret intelligence service is no longer under our control and may be actively working against us! The situation is becoming desperate, and right now you are the best hope we have."

He had made the pitch, the heart of his purpose, and now Gradasov could only wait for the Chief Inspector's reply, although not a hint of the anxiety he felt was evident on his narrow face.

Ever the policeman, Fischer said, "You expect me to share evidence with you, to compromise the case against Lomonosov?"

Gradasov had one card left to play, a card he hoped would resonate with the Chief Inspector's

Michael R. Davidson

ego.

"What we propose is a confidential line of communications directly between you and the President of the Russian Federation. I would be the sole intermediary."

This was flattering to Fischer – he, a policeman, dealing directly with a head of state. It was tempting, but dangerous. This was the realm of diplomats, those beings who swam with confidence in the treacherous sea of international relations. The Chief Inspector had no experience in such deep waters, and yet, the temptation was great – to play at international intrigue at the level of a head of state. Three weeks ago he would never have risked it, risked his pension, his future. The Lomonosov investigation was the well-spring of all the Chief Inspector's recent success, and he dared do nothing to imperil it. But things had changed. A book was now a certainty, and he could envision financial security beyond the reach of the civil service. His part in a back channel to the Russian president would place him among those ephemeral creatures that made history behind the scenes.

"And why should I trust you?"

"There are many kinds of trust, Chief Inspector, and I ask only that you trust yourself. You control the information, and there is nothing we can do to force you to share it. I've explained the stakes."

The Russian was right. Fischer could control the exchange in such a way as to do no harm to the investigation, and perhaps even to enhance it. The name of a high-ranking Russian had been teased out of the encrypted files. This person was completely out of the reach of Swiss law but would serve well to test Gradasov's sincerity. Fischer decided to poke a stick into the wasps' nest and see what happened.

"There is one name."

"Yes?"

"Morozov."

Chapter 23

The Assaf Harofeh Medical Center is located just on the outskirts of Tel Aviv, not far from Ben Gurion International Airport and has a secure wing that handles "private cases" for the Mossad.

Ewan had been treated there for a gunshot wound just the previous year. And now it was Sasha's turn. After a tedious and nerve racking drive to Rome from Switzerland, a heavily bandaged Sasha and the medical team had boarded an El Al flight without incident. Ewan and Ronan had returned to Paris and caught a flight from there. To protect his Irish cover, Ewan had been supplied with Israeli alias documents for the trip.

By the time the two made it to the medical center, Sasha was already in the operating theater where a team of surgeons repaired the damage Dimov had inflicted upon her face. Ewan and Ronan could do nothing but wait, a tedious and uncomfortable experience for two men accustomed to making things happen according to their own timetables.

They retired to the hospital's cafeteria where they sat drinking endless cups of bad coffee. Ronan finally broke the silence. "The doctor said Sasha will require a long convalescence."

"Yes," Ewan replied, "I've been thinking about that."

"Has she told you how we came to know one another?"

"Yes, she has."

Ewan knew the story of how Sasha's father, an immigrant from Russia, had died saving the lives of Ronan and his unit on the Egyptian front during the 1967 war. Ronan had all but adopted the girl and encouraged her fierce desire to emulate him and honor her father.

"I blame myself for this." Ronan waved his arm in a gesture of helplessness that seemed to take in the whole world and cast his eyes down at the table top. His voice was like the distant thunder of a retreating storm.

"I should not have encouraged her to get into this business. She should have been married long ago, had children, and enjoyed working in the garden. That's the proper life for a woman. As it is, I don't think she's ever been truly happy," he paused for a beat and raised his gaze to look Ewan in the eye, "until she met you. Knowing you somehow permitted her to discover a hidden, part of herself, and I think it surprised her as much as it did me."

Ewan had never known the gruff Ronan to express regrets of any sort; he was one of the Mossad's "hard men." But the big man harbored a deep affection for Sasha, and being one used to accepting personal responsibility, he was now heaping censure upon himself. Ewan, too, felt a guilt he knew was entirely irrational for Sasha's ordeal -- an atavistic conviction that men were obliged to protect their women. The two men shared a devotion to the young woman now under the surgeons' knife, a devotion that had until now had pitted them against one another.

"Eitan, don't blame yourself for any of this. Sasha chose her own path, and there was nothing you could have done to prevent it, even if you tried. What's important is that she's safe, and she needs both of us now more than ever."

"I think she will have greater need for you than for me – after what she's been through she needs the kind of reassurance that only a husband or lover can give to a woman."

"I don't intend to leave her side, Eitan, not

ever." He extended his hand across the table. "And I know that you won't either."

*****

Two weeks later, Ewan sat beside Sasha on the hospital's sunny veranda. The doctors had assured them that the operation had gone well and that she could be released any day. The side of her face was still covered in heavy bandages. He had watched them change her dressing, sensing her watching to catch his reaction to her scars, and he had managed to keep his face impassive when the carefully stitched cuts were revealed. Her eyelid had been temporarily sewn shut over the empty socket, but soon she would be fitted with a prosthetic eye. The plastic surgeons had assured them that the scarring, when it healed completely, would be minimal, limited to a tiny hairline. She was taking painkillers and a light tranquillizer, but she was more than ready to leave the antiseptic atmosphere of the hospital.

"Ronan says we can have the house in Caesarea for as long as we need it," he said, knowing this would please her. It had been in that Mossad safehouse by the sea that they had first made love.

"I'd like that," she said. "I can't wait to get

out of here."

It would be a long time before she would be free entirely of medical care. Once her wounds were healed and the stitches removed several weeks of rest and recuperation still would be necessary, and Ewan had an idea.

"Why don't we go to Ireland when they finally let you go? I think a cooler climate and daily gourmet fare prepared by yours truly would do both of us a lot of good, and it's been too long since we've seen Angus. The little bugger is probably fat as a sausage by now and will need some exercise. We could take long walks across the bogs. And we would have a lot of time to practice smooching."

Smiles had been rare and fleeting visitors to Sasha's face, but now one arrived to linger that contained a hint of her old mischievousness.

"I like the sound of that."

Chapter 24

A century after punishment by the knout was abandoned, Russian retribution still is administered with blunt instruments.

Shortly after Anatoliy Gradasov's return to Moscow three men gathered secretly in the Kremlin's venerable Senat building. They were President Yeltsin, Gradasov, and the head of the SVR, Yevgeniy Primakov. The President was engaged in a life or death political battle with the Congress of People's Deputies and his own vice president. Unfortunately, the Zürich distraction only provided more ammunition to his enemies. The new aristocracy of Russia, the "oligarchs," was taking over the economy, and a secret cabal of revanchists was working behind the scenes to pull down all he had worked for. He had neither the time nor the inclination for delicacy. The president's ingestion of vodka had kept pace with the rising tide of crisis that threatened to engulf him, and he was livid. "Morozov? General Morozov of the SVR is involved with these revanchists?"

"The Swiss have proof – his signature on several documents they've decrypted. We have copies."

"Yevgeniy Maksimovich," Yeltsin turned a bloodshot eye to Primakov. "What do you know of this? You're supposed to be in charge of the SVR."

Primakov was a veteran of Kremlin intrigue, but even throughout his long tenure with the KGB he had never encountered a situation so rife with danger, danger that could bring the entire state crashing down around them. His stewardship of the SVR had been difficult, and he had encountered little cooperation as he set about the task of streamlining the organization and bringing it to bear on current priorities. He was resented in the ranks for the wholesale elimination of positions. Hundreds of former KGB officers had been cast out to scrape a living however they might, and many of them had turned to crime as mercenaries or illegal weapons dealers. The intelligence organization had been traumatized and there were few within it that he could trust.

Morozov was the absolute ruler of the powerful Directorate "S", and he had influential political friends on the outside.

"General Morozov is surrounded by a phalanx of protectors. His office is like a fortress, and he tells me only what he thinks he must about his operations. As you know, Mr. President, he also has been working closely with Vitaliy Mikhailovich Shurgin on the weapons sales to the Iranians. Shurgin is the primary liaison with industry in this matter and has met with the Iranian representative, General Hatimi, several times. This relationship is important, given the value of the sales to the Iranians, not to mention the nuclear program."

"So you are telling me that Morozov is untouchable?"

"Not exactly. But if he is, indeed, the head of this group, we must move with care. He undoubtedly controls a large number of SVR officers even beyond his own Department. It could be dangerous."

The President was in no mood for caution. He was a direct man who preferred direct measures, and his alcohol consumption only fueled his impetuosity. "Yevgeniy Maksimovich, I'm preparing the ground to dissolve the Supreme Soviet and the Congress of People's Deputies. This will provoke a constitutional crisis, and I will have my hands full enough without having to worry about the likes of Morozov and his group of renegades. Cut off the head of the snake and the rest will die. That's what I want you to do."

Primakov had always been more of an orthodox diplomat than a wet work type. He believed in the new Russia they were creating and he found the idea of reverting to Stalinist measures repellant.

Yeltsin could see what he was thinking. His own father had been a prisoner in one of Stalin's labor camps, and he had no intention of emulating that Georgian pig.

"No, no, you idiot. I'm not telling you to have him killed. I want you to arrest him and throw him into a cell. Strip him of his rank and privileges, segregate him from his supporters, and let him stew in his own juices. He'll talk soon enough. Then we can weed out his followers."

Primakov still hesitated. "I don't think I can find the people to do this in the SVR. He is highly respected by the rank and file and has a distinguished record."

Yeltsin turned an even darker shade of red, and Gradasov who had sat quietly as the other two argued, stepped in.

"May I make a suggestion, gentlemen? Why not turn to the FSB? Internal security is, after all, their bailiwick."

The FSB, the *Federalnaya Sluzhba Bezopasnosti*, or Federal Security Service, had been recently created from the former Second Chief Directorate of the defunct KGB. They had set up shop in the Lubyanka building that had formerly served as KGB Headquarters.

Primakov, relieved to have the distasteful task passed to someone else, quickly agreed, "That is an excellent suggestion. It would avoid unfortunate, perhaps even violent repercussions at Yasenevo."

Yeltsin stared balefully for a moment longer at Primakov. He had never liked him and had not been enthusiastic about his appointment as SVR Chairman. "Very well," he said with a trace of disgust. "You see to it, Anatoliy. I want this done quietly, mind you."

Primakov and Gradasov rose to leave, but as they reached the door a thought occurred to the President, and he called them back. "Anatoliy, this man Shurgin is a member of the Moscow City Government, is he not?"

"Yes sir. In charge of industrial relations."

"He appears to be important in this Iranian business and working closely with Morozov. I don't want him to be alarmed or confused when Morozov disappears. Arrange a meeting for him with me."

Yeltsin knew that Primakov was a renowned

expert on the Middle East and had been an advocate of the plan to use the Iranians to keep the Americans off balance. Primakov loved these diplomatic dances, and he would resent Yeltsin cutting in. But if the man couldn't be trusted to control his own organization, how could he be trusted to keep this policy on track?

*****

General Morozov had no idea who might be knocking on his apartment door and when he opened it he was confronted by three men dressed in what he immediately recognized as FSB uniforms. Morozov, in his pajamas and robe, stared at them for a moment. "What do you want?" he demanded.

The ranking member of the group was a Lieutenant Colonel. In a polite but firm tone he said, "General Yuriy Ivanovich Morozov, I am instructed to escort you to be questioned."

Morozov blinked in surprise and indignation. "Precisely whose instructions are you following, Colonel? You have no authority over me."

"My orders come from the highest authority, sir." The Colonel's tone did not change. "Please get dressed immediately."

"We'll see about this." Morozov turned from

the door and reached for a telephone on the table in the foyer. To his chagrin he was immediately grabbed by both arms, a man on either side of him, and roughly held in place.

The Colonel lit a cigarette and exhaled noisily. "General Morozov refuses to cooperate, necessitating physical restraint," he said to his two men. "Very well, pajamas will do. Cuff him and bring him to the car."

Morozov's wife, awakened by the noise, opened the bedroom door just in time to see her husband handcuffed and shoved roughly out the door. "Yura," she screamed, "what is happening? What does this mean?"

The General had time only to shout over his shoulder, "Elena, don't worry. It's some kind of mistake." And he disappeared down the corridor, stumbling as the two escorts hurried him along. Some of the neighbors also had been disturbed by the unaccustomed noise in their exclusive apartment building and opened their doors to peek out. When they beheld the uniformed men with the ashen faced, pajama-clad General in tow, they quickly shut them again. A few were old enough to remember the constant dread of a midnight knock on the door during Stalin's reign of terror.

A driver waited for them behind the wheel of a black Mercedes, its motor running, and

Michael R. Davidson

Morozov, who had lost one of his slippers as he was bum rushed through the building, was placed in the rear between the two uniforms. The Lieutenant Colonel sat in the passenger seat beside the driver. *"Poyekhali,* let's go," he said.

His thoughts a kaleidoscope of calculations, Morozov struggled to regain his equilibrium. They had been clever to take him at his apartment, he thought. They would never have been allowed to penetrate to his office. The FSB was responsible for internal security, counter terrorism, and counter-espionage. Morozov had no doubt that his detention was related to the Zürich business – there could really be no other reason. According to the Colonel his detention was on the orders of the "highest authority," and that meant the President or someone close to him. They would never have dared come after him otherwise, and he cursed himself for not having taken more precautions.

The Mercedes made its way north and his spirits sank even lower when he recognized *Matrosskaya Tishina* Street, location of the prison of the same name. This was where the coup plotters of 1991 had been sent for interrogation. He steeled himself for what was to come.

Chapter 25

The day had not begun well or easily for Shurgin. General Morozov had been a no-show at their scheduled meeting at the Moscow safehouse, and calls to his office had failed to locate him. Missing meetings and absenteeism were foreign to the highly disciplined SVR General. Shurgin hoped there was a good explanation, and fought against a mounting sense of unease. He recalled Morozov's behavior at their last meeting, the impression he had given of losing confidence in *Voskreseniye's* ultimate success.

Shurgin had to admit to himself that Morozov had borne the lion's share of operational responsibility as they had carried out their plans. It was important to Shurgin to keep his name out of it all. The General had recruited the network inside the SVR and negotiated the mutually beneficial agreement with Zhenya and the *Bratsvo*. They had been confident that Morozov was bulletproof so long as he controlled the powerful Directorate "S". But Zürich changed everything. Zhenya might have been a highly proficient, if brutal criminal, but he had had no sense of the discipline required for sensitive intelligence operations. The deceased *vor v zakonye* evidently had been sloppy with incriminating documents and information, no doubt secure in the ultimately *mistaken* belief that his compound was impenetrable. His carelessness had put them all in danger.

There would be repercussions as the Western authorities worked their way through the files and inevitably leaked details to the media. There had been only three people aware of the full extent of *Voskreseniye*-SVR-*Bratsvo* operations: Shurgin, Morozov, and Zhenya. And now one of them was dead and another missing. He wondered if he would be next.

Shurgin had returned to his office at the City Administration and was considering whether it would be prudent to make a call to Morozov's apartment when his ruminations were interrupted by his secretary who informed him that a man from the Presidency was on the line.

Was this the other shoe dropping? He picked

up the telephone with some trepidation. The caller introduced himself as Anatoliy Gradasov, a senior advisor to the President. He wondered if Shurgin could present himself at the Kremlin that afternoon for a private meeting. There would be a pass waiting for him at the Borovitskiy entrance.

It was an invitation he couldn't refuse.

Deciding that it would do him no good to arrive at the Kremlin in his chauffeured official limousine, he had his driver drop him at home where he retrieved his own more modest BMW 3-series, and an hour later he drove slowly across the Bol'shoy Kamenniy Bridge, the bulk of the Kremlin rising on his right across the Moscow River brilliant in the afternoon sunlight. He passed under the arch of the red brick Borovitskiy Tower and the guard directed him to continue driving parallel to the inside of the Kremlin wall and park in Ivanonvskaya Square in front of the Chudov Monastery, or "Monastery of Miracles." Shurgin could use a miracle now. He was accustomed to controlling events, but now found himself passing through a vertiginous landscape of uncertainty where any misstep could be fatal.

The *Senat* is an unusual building, originally commissioned by Catherine the Great, its triangular exterior concealing the magnificent yellow and white Rotunda Hall that dominates the inner courtyard. Vladimir Lenin had once inhabited an apartment here. But none of this mattered to Shurgin as he crossed the space leading to the entrance of the Presidential offices.

Alerted by the guard, Gradasov waited to receive him just inside the door. "Mr. Shurgin, so nice of you to make time for us on such short notice. President Yeltsin is anxious to meet you."

Shurgin's calm exterior betrayed none of his inner turmoil. Fear was an uncommon emotion for him. "Your call was a surprise. I can't imagine why the President would want to see me."

"I'll leave it to him to tell you," Gradasov smiled as he led the visitor through a maze of ornate beige-carpeted corridors and up a flight stairs to the anteroom just outside the Presidential suite. Gradasov disappeared through the huge double doors and stuck his head out a moment later to beckon Shurgin to join him.

Swallowing the bile that had risen in his throat, he walked through the doors.

Chapter 26

Yeltsin, in shirtsleeves and with his tie loosened, waited on a sofa near the window. He rose, a bit unsteadily, when they entered. There was a politician's smile on his broad, Siberian face, but his eyes as they raked across his visitor were calculating.

Gradasov introduced them, and the President waved them over to sit with him in the comfortable suite by the window. Light from the early afternoon sun sparkled on a carafe that sat surrounded by small glasses on a tray on the table between them, and Shurgin wondered whether it contained water or vodka. He had seen the President before at official functions but had never had occasion to have a conversation with him. He waited for the man to speak.

"You oversee industry for the Moscow region, I understand."

"Yes, Mr. President."

What he didn't say was that he, in fact, *owned* or financially controlled major industries throughout the entire country, although his participation was carefully hidden behind so-called "oligarchs," financed with *Voskreseniye* money.

"And you have been instrumental in our relations with the Iranians."

It was a statement, not a question.

"Yes, Mr. President."

"You have worked closely with General Morozov of the SVR."

Another statement. *Now we're getting to it,* he thought. *Don't volunteer anything.*

"There has been an unfortunate development involving the General." Yeltsin was still watching him closely with those small, shrewd peasant eyes. "I thought it best to inform you directly to avoid any ... misunderstanding."

"An 'unfortunate development'?" *This could mean anything.*

"I won't play mind games with you. Shurgin. I'm a plain man, and I speak plainly. The General was detained last night for questioning in connection with crimes against the state. He's been placed in *Matrosskaya Tishina.*"

Shurgin permitted an expression of mild surprise to appear on his foxlike face. *Morozov had been arrested. How will that affect me?*

"I've known General Morozov for a long time, Mr. President," he chose his words carefully. "As you may know, we came up through the ranks together in the KGB. I've never known him to be disloyal." *This was a safe statement, supportive of a colleague but totally neutral.*

Maybe there was a chance that Morozov could be salvaged.

The President's face screwed into a sour expression, his eyes narrowed to slits. "The KGB – the 'sword and shield of the Revolution,' I think was the old motto. I fear that your old comrade was thinking of skewering the heart of our new Russia with that sword."

Yeltsin leaned forward and pointed a fat finger at Shurgin. "What do you know of his traitorous actions at the SVR, Shurgin?"

Did he know something, or was he fishing? Had Morozov said something? Regardless, there was only one possible response. Affecting wounded pride, Shurgin answered, "I've been out of the intelligence trade for a long time, for almost three years. I'm a complete outsider now, and I know nothing of what might be happening on the inside, especially since the reorganization. As you said, my contact with General Morozov of late has been limited entirely to our work with the Iranians."

Yeltsin sank back into the sofa's cushions with a grunt, his face inscrutable. No one spoke for several moments as Shurgin waited for whatever was to come next.

At last, the President spoke again. "The SVR cannot be trusted, Shurgin. I no longer have confidence in them to carry out the missions they are assigned, and that includes the Iranian matter. We'll correct that situation, but for the time being an SVR man can no longer be in charge of that delicate relationship. My enemies would rather see the country descend into anarchy than have my Administration succeed. And I have many enemies. Are you one of them, Shurgin?"

"I'm dedicated to building a new Russia, sir, a democratic Russia with a thriving economy." Shurgin injected fervor into his voice. "That is why I've devoted my energies to rebuilding our industrial sector."

Yeltsin's eyes seemed to focus on something far away as he reached a decision. He again shifted to the front of the sofa, stretched a meaty hand for the carafe, and poured three glasses of the crystal liquid. "Drink with me, Shurgin. I'm appointing you in charge of the entire Iranian matter."

Barely able to restrain his hand from trembling, Shurgin took the proffered glass and downed the vodka in unison with Yeltsin and Gradasov.

Fifteen minutes later he was back in his car gliding through the gates under the Borovitskiy Tower and back out into traffic. The tension from the interview with Yeltsin drained away as he left the walls of the Kremlin behind and he felt suddenly exhausted. He had to blink several times before his eyes would focus properly.

He was safe – for now. Once again he cursed Zhenya and hoped the tattooed bastard was burning in hell. The *Voskreseniye* organization was crumbling, and the *vor v zakonye*'s incompetence was the proximate cause.

He decided to go to his office at the Moscow City Government building and steered the car across Borovitskaya Square and then north on Mokhovaya toward Novy Arbat. Once inside the skyscraper that housed the municipal offices, he ascended the elevator to his office. He was pleased to see nothing abnormal. His staff was working quietly, and his secretary told him there had been no calls.

Immediate concerns mollified, he now turned his thoughts to the most pressing threat to his continued well-being – Morozov. He maintained excellent contacts inside the FSB, and as things stood there remained only one certain way to avoid danger.

*****

Prison garb had replaced the pajamas and robe he had been wearing when they had taken him. He had not been physically mistreated, although they had shown him very little respect either. The evidence against him looked considerable and convincing. They had shown him incriminating documents bearing his own signature that they said guaranteed that he would be convicted of crimes against the state. They had appealed to his patriotism, and at this he had shouted at them that they didn't know what the word meant. After three days, of questioning the General still refused to give the interrogators what they wanted.

Morozov believed in the goals of *Voskreseniye*. He considered himself a patriot combating a corrupt regime that was dragging his beloved Russia through the mud. If all the FSB had was documents linking him to Zhenya Lomonosov, the rest of *Voskreseniye* might still be safe. He would never betray Shurgin any more than he would betray Mother Russia, and he hoped against hope that his friend would find a way to extricate him. There was a large numbered bank account controlled by a trusted financier in Monaco on which he and his family could live out the rest of their lives in comfort.

The morning of the fourth day of incarceration two guards came to fetch him from his cell, and he stood and extended his arms behind so they could cuff his hands before he was led out for another session in the interrogation room. As the cuffs snapped around his wrists he noted a curious expression cross the face of the second guard, a wary look of anticipation. At the same instant the guard at his back slipped a knotted garrote over his head and yanked it tight around his throat.

Morozov's eyes bulged in surprise and he tried to cry out, but the cord completely cut off his air supply. With his arms bound he was next to helpless, and the second guard quickly dove to hold his thrashing legs. He struggled nevertheless, but as happens with all strangling victims there came the heartrending realization that there would be no escape – that he was going to die here in this squalid prison basement.

He went rigid and finally slack as life slipped from him, and the two guards let his body slump to the floor. They quickly went to work fashioning a noose from a sheet from the cell's narrow cot and strung it over a hook high up on the wall, a grisly relic of Stalin's time. Lifting Morozov's heavy body with an effort, they placed the noose around his neck and hoisted him up until the twisted sheet supported his weight. They stood back a few seconds to check the scene – the General was a big man and they didn't want the sheet to tear. Satisfied, they turned and strode out of the cell, locking the door behind them.

Later that morning Shurgin received a call on his private line. The caller uttered only a single word, "*Zdelano*, done," before hanging up.

Shurgin carefully replaced the receiver and an expression that might be interpreted as sadness flashed for an instant across his sharp features and then was gone. He turned back to the papers on his desk. He had a lot of work to do.

Chapter 27

CAESAREA

"It's five o'clock," announced Ewan as he crossed the veranda's broad expanse carefully balancing a tray upon which stood three large martini glasses filled to the brim with his own mixture of gin and a dash of vermouth and some large olives.

Sasha and Ronan had arranged themselves in cushioned chairs around a table and were enjoying the failing rays of the sun as it sank into the Mediterranean burnishing the surface of the sea to a rosy sheen. The dressings had at last been removed from Sasha's face which still displayed some slight swelling and bruising from her surgeries. The stitches had been removed a

Michael R. Davidson

week earlier, and the doctors assured them that scarring would, in the end, be minimal. Her destroyed eye had been replaced with a prosthesis to which she was still adapting, and she occasionally wore an eye patch.

Regardless of the physical reminders of her ordeal, her mood had improved since her release from the hospital. Ewan was taking it slowly, grateful she was alive and that they were together. The villa in Caesarea brought back pleasant memories and, for once, there was no pressure from the Mossad for debriefings and post-mortems. David Shalev had seen to that.

At first she had suffered nightly terrors that invaded her dreams, and he had held her for hours in the darkness until the trembling subsided. They had not yet made love, but it was clear that she needed his touch, needed to be near him. The nightmare of her torture would remain a burden she must carry forever, but she was resilient, and her strength was returning.

Ronan was a frequent visitor, and had become very solicitous of both Sasha and Ewan. Their joint rescue of Sasha had given him a new respect for the American and a complete appreciation for his relationship with Sasha. Having concluded that they were a pair, an inseparable unit, he had correspondingly adapted.

Ewan was now a true comrade in arms and a friend.

The big Israeli dubiously eyed the ice cold concoction that Ewan had placed before him in the stemmed glass. He would never get used to a drink that for some dark and mysterious reason had a green olive lurking at the bottom ready to choke him. Ronan preferred beer to all other alcoholic beverages but acceded to Ewan's invitation to join them in what had become a five o'clock ritual.

"If I drink this thing I won't be able to drive back to Tel Aviv tonight," he grumbled.

"Wonderful," Sasha smiled, a beautiful thing to Ronan, "Then you'll have a few more and spend the night. Marnie is preparing a wonderful dinner, and we'll have more drinks after. You can always drive back tomorrow after breakfast."

Marnie and her husband Moshe were the safehouse keepers.

Ewan was smiling too. He knew that Ronan detested martinis and therefore delighted in plying him with one at every opportunity. "That's a great idea, Sasha! We'll make a night of it – the Three Musketeers." He raised his glass, "One for all, and all for one!"

Ronan tipped the odious beverage to his lips and it dribbled over the side of the stemmed, conical glass that was designed for judicious sipping. He just couldn't get used to sipping.

The complaint that rose to his lips was instantly stifled by Sasha's giggle, which brought a grin instead to his face. "I'll pour the whole damned thing on my head, and stick the olive up my nose, if it pleases you," he said to her with mock severity.

"There's a punishment for wasting gin like that," said Ewan with a malicious grin. "You'll have to have another martini."

"I solemnly promise to sip."

The two were leaving for Ireland the following week after a final medical appointment for Sasha, and Ronan knew he was going to miss seeing them so often.

"Just promise to come see us in Ireland," Sasha said.

Ronan agreed, but everyone knew it would not be easy. Once they left Israel, it would be back to the grindstone for him. Israel's enemies did not rest. "One of these days I'll show up there with another job, and you won't be so pleased to see me," he said.

He and Ewan had discussed when they might be ready for another operation, and they had agreed that this would only happen when Ewan was certain Sasha could handle it. Neither knew how long that might be.

They had also puzzled out the ramifications of the operation that had brought them to this juncture. For a second time they had encountered *Voskreseniye* and triumphed, but at a terrible price.

Chapter 28

IRELAND

The Land Rover rolled to a halt on the narrow dirt track, and the passenger side door opened to permit the joyfully enthusiastic exit of a somewhat round in the belly black Scots Terrier. Without hesitation he plunged off into the heather that covered Roundstone Bog, nose twitching. After a moment only the erect point of his tail was visible as he tore through the underbrush in search of plover.

Ewan Ramsay alighted from the driver's side and went around to help Sasha out of the SUV. It was a spectacular late summer day in Connemara, and they had packed a picnic lunch to enjoy in the bog land where Angus could roam freely to his heart's content.

Dressed in jeans and one of Ewan's old shirts Sasha was beautiful in the sunlight. Her long blond hair now parted on the right so it hung over the left side of her face was radiant as ever. Her scars had healed leaving only a hairline in her eyebrow and cheek, and she had adjusted well to the artificial eye but was still self-conscious about it. She was regaining her old vigor, and he no longer worried that a trek across the bog might tire her too much.

Autumn was around the corner, and in a few months, the bog lands and the sea would assume a different character as winter enveloped them, and the gales beat in from the sea against the stone walls of the house that protected the souls within.

THE END

Michael R. Davidson

The Author

Michael R. Davidson was raised in the Mid-West. Heeding President Kennedy's call for more young Americans to learn Russian he studied the language, and military service took him to the White House where he served as translator for the Moscow-Washington "Hotline." His language abilities attracted the attention of the Central Intelligence Agency, and following his military service Mr. Davidson spent the next 28 years as a Clandestine Services officer. Seventeen of those years were spent abroad in a variety of sensitive posts working against the Soviet Union and the Warsaw Pact. In the private sector he worked as a business owner and security and economic development consultant before devoting full time to his writing.

Also by Michael R. Davidson

The RESURRECTION Series

Did the Cold War end or did the KGB find a way to retain its power and dominate the new Russian Federation? "Harry's Rules" is an espionage thriller set against the backdrop of post-Soviet Russia in the early 1990's.

Who killed President John F. Kennedy? A long buried secret that could change the course of history draws murder to a quiet Washington suburb. Only an exiled CIA officer can solve a mystery that both the White House and the Kremlin will protect at all costs.

Revenge is said to be a dish best served cold. A suicide bomber and a serial killer are the instruments chosen by a deposed Russian president.

But his targets are anything but helpless.

Find them all at: www.michaelrdavidson.com

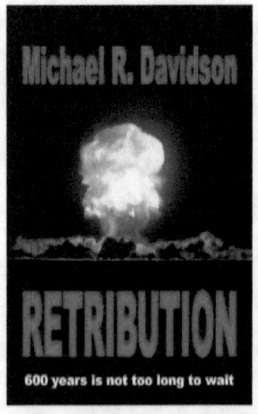

KRYSTAL - **Sassy** Detective Krystal Murphy who appeared in INCUBUS and THE INCUBUS VENDETTA at last gets her own novel.

A controversial Miami judge is murdered in a Washington hotel room. Homicide detective Krystal Murphy identifies an ideal suspect, a person with motive and opportunity. Following the suspect's trail to Miami, she is confronted by an unspeakable tragedy that leaves her prime suspect dead. Convinced her initial instincts were wrong and driven by guilt, she teams with a Miami detective to continue the investigation. But she encounters unexpected opposition from her own superiors who want only to call the case closed. While coping with her own personal tragedy and under great pressure from her superiors, Krystal doggedly pursues the case with the help a new ally and perhaps more than just a friend, the Miami detective. When more people associated with the case begin turning up dead, Krystal finds herself in a race against time before she herself becomes the next victim of an increasingly desperate killer.

Find them all at: www.michaelrdavidson.com

Michael R. Davidson

www.ingramcontent.com/pod-product-compliance
Lightning Source LLC
Chambersburg PA
CBHW050939120626
46552CB00001B/295